THE DARING GAME

Born in Edmonton, Alberta, Kit Pearson graduated in English at the University of Alberta before going on to get her MLS at the University of British Columbia and an MA in children's literature at the Center for the Study of Children's Literature, Simmons College, Boston.

A former librarian as well as a writer, Ms Pearson has written several novels, including *The Daring Game*, *A Handful of Time* and a trilogy consisting of *The Sky Is Falling*, *Looking at the Moon* and *The Lights Go On Again*. Her most recent novel, *Awake and Dreaming*, won the Governor General's Award for Children's Literature.

Lindsay

Schieck

THE
DARING
GAME

Kit Pearson

Puffin Books

PUFFIN BOOKS
Published by the Penguin Group
Penguin Books Canada Ltd, 10 Alcorn Avenue, Toronto, Ontario, Canada
M4V 3B2
Penguin Books Ltd, 27 Wrights Lane, London W8 5TZ, England
Penguin Putnam Inc., 375 Hudson Street, New York, New York 10014,
U.S.A.
Penguin Books Australia Ltd, Ringwood, Victoria, Australia
Penguin Books (NZ) Ltd, cnr Rosedale and Airborne Roads, Albany,
Auckland 1310, New Zealand

Penguin Books Ltd, Registered Offices: Harmondsworth, Middlesex,
England

First published by Penguin Books Canada Limited, 1986
Published in Puffin Books, 1987

20

*Publisher's note: This book is a work of fiction. Names, characters, places and inci-
dents either are the product of the author's imagination or are used fictitiously, and
any resemblance to actual persons living or dead, events, or locales is entirely coin-
cidental.*

Manufactured in Canada

Canadian Cataloguing in Publication Data
Pearson, Kit, 1947-
The daring game

ISBN 0-14-031932-8

I. Title

PS8581.E27D37 1987   jC813'.54   C85-099356-3
PZ7.P42Da 1987

Visit Penguin Canada's web site at **www.penguin.ca**

Acknowledgements

The hymns and carols that Eliza sings are from
The Book of Common Praise,
Toronto, Oxford University Press, 1962.

The poem Eliza hears Miss Tavistock reading is
"Invictus," written by William Ernest Henley in 1875.

"Norman" by John D. Loudermilk
© 1961 by Acuff-Rose Publications, Inc.
Used by permission of the publisher. All rights reserved.

"Ashdown Academy" is modelled after a school
I once knew very well. I was older than Eliza when I
attended it, however, and none of the students or
staff of that school are portrayed in this novel.
It is a work of fiction.

"Semper Fideles"
("Always Faithful")

Ashdown Academy motto

For Joe and Anne Pearson
and for
the Class of '65

Contents

Part I
Fall

I

Ashdown Academy

Eliza sat alone in the headmistress's study, trying to stop her knees from trembling. Tugging her dress over them, she wondered again if she should have worn her uniform.

She didn't want to begin boarding school with any mistakes. It was bad enough having to start a day late because her uncle's car had broken down on their camping trip. She slipped off one shoe and swung it from her big toe nervously. Perhaps her white knee socks weren't correct either; did grade seven girls in Vancouver wear socks or nylons?

Taking a steadying breath, Eliza looked around the room. An oak desk beside her was covered with orderly piles of papers. A daily calendar stood beside them, and her own name leaped out at her in upside-down precise writing: "September 6, 1964 — Elizabeth Chapman 11 a.m."

On one wall of the crowded study was an oil painting of a stern-looking woman with frizzy grey hair. Eliza stared at her face, trying to imagine it relaxing into a smile. She listened to the rattle of the rain on the veranda roof and the even *tock tock* of a clock in the hall.

"Ah, Elizabeth." The brisk voice brought Eliza to her feet with a start, fitting on her shoe hastily.

"I'm so sorry to be late. How do you do? I am Miss Tavistock." The tall angular woman looked so much like the one in the picture that, for a second, Eliza thought she was dreaming. But Miss Tavistock had brown hair, not grey, and her firm handshake was very real.

Shutting the door, the headmistress pulled a chair from behind the desk to face Eliza. "Please sit down. I'm delighted to finally meet you after we've both been delayed."

"My aunt and uncle were sorry they couldn't stay," said Eliza, her voice croaking. "The baby started crying and they had to take her home." Then she remembered another message. "And Mum and Dad said to say they were sorry they had to go to Toronto so early and couldn't come with me to meet you."

"Yes, I had a very nice letter from your mother explaining it all. At least we've got *you* here, and that's the most important thing. Welcome to Ashdown, Elizabeth. I hope you'll be happy this year."

The headmistress's huge, deep blue eyes, the only round feature in her bony face, looked kind. Eliza began to relax slightly. "You can call me Eliza," she ventured.

"We believe in proper names here," said Miss Tavistock, in a tone which didn't expect any arguments. "And Elizabeth is such a beautiful one," she added more gently.

Eliza wasn't sure she liked this; she was never called by her full name. But she didn't seem to have a choice.

"I've asked for some tea, so we can get acquainted," said Miss Tavistock. "Now tell me what you think of Vancouver."

Eliza sat up straighter. "I think it's . . . really nice." It sounded so lame. She wished she could express how attached she already felt to this city. Vancouver made the Alberta prairies look drab. The mountains that rose straight out of the bay surprised her continually; their massive, tree-covered shapes were a different shade of blue each morning.

She was shyly describing the beach on Vancouver Island where they'd gone camping, when a tray with a silver teapot on it was passed around the door by invisible hands. The headmistress poured Eliza a cup without even asking if she wanted it.

"Just milk? There you are. Now let me tell you about Ashdown. The other girls are all at church. We go to the cathedral every Sunday, but I went to the early service at St Mary's so I could meet you. They'll be back in about an hour. You will be in the Yellow Dormitory with four others — Caroline Olsen,

Pamela Jennings, Jean McQuiggan and Helen Beauchamp. They're all new boarders like yourself, except for Helen. She's been with us for three years now."

She paused, and Eliza thought she gave a slight sigh, but then she continued. "I've put the five of you together because you're the youngest of the grade sevens — two of you are still eleven."

Eliza nibbled on a chocolate-covered cookie as she stopped listening and tried to remember those four names.

". . . and the school was founded in 1910 by my great-aunt, Miss Dora Peck. She's still alive, although she's very old — that's her picture."

So that was why they looked alike. Eliza tried to concentrate on balancing her cup, saucer, cookie and napkin on her lap as Miss Tavistock told her the aims of Ashdown Academy. There seemed to be a lot of them.

". . . and, most important of all, whenever there is a conflict between one's personal desires and the general good, I hope that an Ashdown student would choose the school over herself." The headmistress paused and looked expectantly at her. Eliza's knees wobbled and she spilled tea on her dress. She knows I'm not paying attention, she thought unhappily.

"Well, I'm sure you won't have any difficulty living up to Ashdown's standards, Elizabeth," said Miss Tavistock with a quick smile. "Now, you probably would like to have a little quiet time in your dormitory before the others return." She pressed a buzzer. "Miss Monaghan will show you where everything is."

Before Eliza knew what was happening she was out the door, her sloppy cup and saucer retrieved from her and her dress wiped by Miss Tavistock without a word. The first ordeal was over.

"I don't have much time, you know. I have to be out of here in ten minutes. She certainly kept you long." Eliza hurried up the stairs behind Miss Monaghan, straining to catch her words. They passed the open doors of rooms cluttered with suitcases, turned down a narrow hall and went into a square room with windows across three of its yellow walls.

"Here we are — this is your dorm. It looks like they've left you the upper bunk, I'm afraid. Here's your dresser and your suitcase. You can start putting your clothes away. The closet's here, and your dorm has its own bathroom."

The matron led Eliza back into the hall. "Look, here's your hook, with your towel and washcloth on it." She pointed to a closed door across from the bathroom. "Your matron sleeps next door."

"Aren't *you* my matron?" Eliza asked, as she was whisked from the bathroom into the dorm again.

"Me? Oh no, I'm the school nurse, and I also take care of the juniors. We're on the top floor. Your matron is Miss Bixley. You'll like her — she and I aren't as fussy as some of the others."

Miss Monaghan had an odd, twanging accent. "Are you English?" Eliza asked her.

The matron shook her mop of hair vigorously. "Heavens, no, I'm an Aussie! Over here for a few years to see your beautiful country. Now I really must be off. It's my half-day and I'm meeting some friends downtown. Will you be all right by yourself? The others will be back soon." Eliza nodded, and the energetic young woman almost ran down the hall.

Eliza climbed up onto her bed. It slumped in the middle but had a good view. She didn't mind sleeping up here. It made her feel safe, being so high above the floor.

The Yellow Dorm. *Her* dorm. The room looked much as she had imagined it: four narrow beds pushed against the walls, one with her bunk above it. They were neatly made with worn blue bedspreads. Stuffed animals — a bushy white dog and a purple hippo — were perched on two of them. So *that* was all right. Eliza hopped down, opened her suitcase and pulled out John, her small furless bear, whom she had hidden under her clothes. She positioned him carefully on her pillow and immediately felt more at home.

She walked around and looked at everyone's things. A sheaf of bright ribbons was knotted together and fanned across someone's dresser. Someone else had a tennis racquet and a mysterious-looking curved stick lying on her bed. On the pillow with the dog on it lay *The Incredible Journey*, a book Eliza had read many times.

The bed under hers had a string of nametapes strewn over it; a uniform blouse had been abandoned in the middle of sewing one on. "Helen Beauchamp," the tapes said. Eliza felt sorry for this person. All her own clothes were neatly labelled. It had been a mistake to use her full name, although now that Miss Tavistock was calling her by it, it seemed appropriate. "Elizabeth Norah Chapman" in Cash's Woven Nametapes was two-and-a-half inches long. Stitching each strip into place on every sock and piece of underwear was an endless task, and Eliza's mother had ended up doing most of them herself.

Eliza looked at her watch — twenty more minutes. She might as well unpack. First she put on her dresser the picture her mother had framed for her: Mum, Dad and the Demons, smiling in the snow. They were in Toronto now, unpacking in *their* new place. Unexpected tears swelled in Eliza's eyes, but she blinked them away. "Silly," she told herself, "you *wanted* to come here."

She stuck a photograph of Jessie under the frame of the dresser mirror. The golden labrador's adoring eyes gazed out at her. To stop more tears, Eliza shifted her glance to her own face instead.

The back-to-school haircut she had just had was too short: her straight light brown hair looked ridiculous, like an inverted bowl on her head. She examined her grey eyes and snubby nose nervously. The others would probably think she looked really young.

Tumbling her clothes helter-skelter into the drawers, Eliza shut them with a bang and clambered onto her bed again. If only the time would go faster. The longer she waited for her new dorm-mates to arrive, the more frightened she became. What if she didn't

like them? Or, worse, what if they didn't like her?
Leaning back against her pillow with John in her
arms, she tried to think of something else.

She had always wanted to go to boarding school. Her
English grandmother had sent her many books over
the years with titles like *Fiona of the Fifth* or *The Tur-
bulent Term at St Theresa's*. They depicted a dramatic world of odd rituals, ordered busyness and loyal
friends. Of course, a Canadian boarding school might
be different, but there must be some similarities.

Her mother had said that Eliza might be able
to go away to school in grade ten. There was a girls'
school in Vancouver with an excellent reputation.
Her father, however, wasn't so sure; he thought private schools were snobbish.

"Am I a snob?" Mum teased him. "After all, I
went to one in Toronto." But Dad would only say
that, although he wanted Eliza to have a good educa-
tion, they had lots of time before they even had to consider it.

Then Eliza's father, who was an ophthalmo-
gist, had been asked to help start an eye clinic at the
Toronto General Hospital. They were all supposed
to move east for a year: Eliza, her parents and the
Demons, her two-year-old twin brothers. Her mother
was excited about going back to the city where she'd
grown up and where her parents still lived; her father
had been waiting for an opportunity like this for years.

But Eliza didn't want to go. For weeks she had

fought a campaign to go to Ashdown Academy in Vancouver instead.

"You're much too young," her parents both said at once. "You'll be terribly homesick and we'll miss you too much."

"I'm *not* too young," insisted Eliza. Some of the girls in her books were even younger than eleven. "Of course we'll miss each other, but it's only for a year. And Aunt Susan and Uncle Adrian are there. And I would have had to change schools this year anyway."

She didn't tell them how the prospect of attending the huge junior high school terrified her. Eliza didn't want to become a teenager. She was the youngest, although the tallest, in her class, and all her friends were changing. Already they were talking about movie stars and backcombing and dating.

"Eliza, sweetheart, are you sure it's not because of the twins?" her mother asked anxiously. Eliza sighed. Ever since the Demons had been born, she'd had to keep convincing her parents she wasn't jealous of them. She loved her brothers, but she wished they would hurry up and become normal people instead of two screaming tornadoes who kept getting into her room. She couldn't tell her mother it would be a rest to be away from them for a while.

She argued and argued, and finally her parents agreed. "I don't know how I'll last so long without you, Lizabel," said her father, "but maybe you'll get it out of your system if we let you go now. And at least you have Adrian and Susan to keep an eye on you."

"If you're the least bit unhappy you must let us know at once," said her mother.

They had to apply right away. Eliza wrote the entrance exam in the principal's office at her elementary school and was accepted two weeks later. Then the clothing list arrived. She pored over it for hours.

1 regulation grey pleated skirt
6 regulation blue blouses
1 navy-blue blazer
6 pairs of navy-blue knee socks
3 pairs of navy-blue bloomers
1 pair of black oxford shoes
1 navy-blue gabardine raincoat
1 regulation blue beret
1 grey V-neck sweater
2 pairs of navy-blue gloves
1 pair of white gloves

This certainly sounded like her books. The requirements continued for pages and included items she'd never owned before — a sewing basket, a shoe-shining kit and an umbrella.

Eliza's mother laughed at the bloomers. "I haven't heard of those for years!" They ordered the uniform from a store in Vancouver. When it arrived, Eliza tried everything on and examined herself in the hall mirror.

She looked like one of the girls in the illustrations in her English books — very neat, all grey and blue. Eliza liked things that matched, and blue was her favourite colour. The bloomers, which were like long serge shorts with gathered bottoms, were soft and cosy. The black lace-up shoes were ugly, but felt secure and substantial on her feet. "I'm going to Ashdown," she said importantly to her reflection.

August flashed by in a blur of packing and good-byes. The Chapmans had to be in Toronto by the beginning of September. Aunt Susan arrived with her new baby to help pack and to take Eliza back to Vancouver. Eliza's parents had taken the train east the same day she and her aunt had taken it west.

Now she heard two buses pull up below the window, and she instantly wished this time alone wasn't about to end. She hid behind the curtains and watched as a chattering swarm of girls emerged from the buses and spread out onto the pavement. From above they looked like a sea of coats, light blue berets bobbing on navy-blue waves.

Half the crowd melted around the corner; Eliza assumed they were the seniors, whom she knew lived in a separate building. The rest advanced towards her, and she hid even farther back. At once the quiet old house was filled with high voices and thumping feet.

The din grew louder as it came up the stairs to the second floor. One set of footsteps pounded quickly down the hall, followed by slower ones, and a mild voice calling, "Walk, please, Helen."

Eliza turned and faced the door.

II

The Yellow Dorm

The clamour stopped. Four pairs of curious eyes and four motionless bodies surrounded her. The first thing she noticed, with relief, was that they all wore socks.

A small woman with wispy yellowy-white hair stepped around from behind them. "Now girls, don't stare at poor Eliza like that. Eliza, these are your dorm-mates — Carrie, Pam, Jean and Helen. I'm Miss Bixley. We're so glad you finally got here. I'll leave you all now to get acquainted."

Then they crowded her even more. I'm the tallest, Eliza thought frantically. I'm not afraid.

"Nice to meet you," said Pam, pulling her white gloves off one long finger at a time. Her hands were smooth and tanned, and each nail was filed into a perfect arc. She examined Eliza coolly. Eliza at once felt babyish in her short tartan dress.

Jean smiled timidly, revealing a mouth full of braces, but she looked as if she wanted to run away and hide.

Helen sent her beret skimming across the room. Eliza shrank as the other girl stepped closer and peered at her. She resembled an angry owl. Her round face was chalk-white, and her short hair stood straight up in rusty red tufts. The large circles of her glasses made Eliza feel as if Helen could see right inside her.

"Well, well, well . . . so you're Eliza. Welcome to prison."

Eliza didn't know what to reply to this. She turned with gratitude to the beaming fourth girl, Carrie, who had a heavy blond braid hanging down her back. "Oh, Eliza, I'm so glad you're here! Now we're really complete. You're from Edmonton, aren't you? I'm from Seattle."

"If there's anything you want to know, just ask me," said Pam. "I'm the dorm head."

"Only because you and I are the only two old girls, and I didn't want to do it," retorted Helen.

Pam ignored this. "I was a day-girl last year, but my father was transferred to Geneva for a year. That's in Switzerland, you know."

"If you don't want the top bunk I'll trade with you," offered Carrie.

Eliza knew she should respond to the volley of comments that were being hurled at her, but her tongue seemed glued to the roof of her mouth, and words wouldn't come out of her parched throat. All she could manage was to stand there foolishly and try to smile.

Miss Bixley bustled back in. "Helen, you have time before lunch to sew on some more nametapes. Come on, I'll help you."

"Miss Bixley," said Pam, "shouldn't Eliza put on her Sunday uniform?"

"Oh, that's not necessary, not when she'd just be changing out of it again after lunch."

Eliza found her voice: "Please, couldn't I?" It would be terrible to be the only one at lunch not in uniform.

"Very well, if you really want to. On Sundays you wear your white blouse, navy-blue pleated skirt and blazer. The black pumps you have on will be fine."

Too late, Eliza realized that now she'd have to change in front of all these eyes. But each girl became occupied with something in her own corner of the room, although they still kept throwing her information.

"We aren't allowed to wear nylons until eighth grade," said Carrie, knotting a white ribbon carefully on the end of her braid.

"We can on Saturdays, though," said Pam. "On Saturdays and in the evenings we can wear whatever we want — as long as it's a skirt. And on Sunday afternoons we can wear slacks."

Helen glowered from the midst of her nametapes. "Clothes, clothes, that's all you ever think about, P.J." She jabbed her needle into her blouse, then thrust her thumb into her mouth with a curse. Jean looked up from her book fearfully.

Pam turned pink. "Don't call me P.J. — I don't like it!"

"Now you two, stop your bickering," said Miss Bixley calmly. "Here, Helen, give me that — you're getting blood all over it."

CLANG A CLANG A CLANG A CLANG A CLANG! Eliza jumped as someone downstairs rang a handbell vigorously. Its harsh metal voice vibrated painfully in her ears.

"Sunday dinner! The best meal of the week!" Helen pushed past her and ran out of the dorm.

"Come on, Eliza!" Eliza quickly turned her blouse collar over her blazer collar, so she looked like the others, and followed Carrie down the corridor.

At lunch she was relieved to find herself assigned to the same table as Carrie. Trying to make herself invisible, she watched an older girl at the head of the table carve the roast efficiently. Then the senior introduced Eliza to everyone. Eliza didn't say a word, just gulped down her meat and vegetables hungrily when they were allowed to begin. Five long tables of boarders around her kept up such a roar of conversation that it was easy to remain silent.

After lunch they all trooped up and down the stairs many times, carrying the contents of their trunks from the veranda to the dorms. When they had finished putting everything away, Eliza and Carrie went outside to explore. It had finally stopped raining, but their feet got soaked as they trekked through the wet grass.

It was hard to believe Ashdown was in the middle of a large city. Its spacious grounds, almost entirely bordered by a stone wall blanketed in ivy, made it a hidden retreat from the busy streets outside.

"Look at all the trees!" Eliza ran across the lawn away from the Old Residence. They had made a circular tour of the low school building, the white gym with its four pillars and the sleek New Residence. The latter they had tiptoed by, their ears wide open to the buzz of the seniors drifting through its open windows.

Eliza scrambled easily up the broad red branches of an arbutus, wondering if Carrie would think she was too old to climb trees. But the other girl just watched her calmly. "Let's go down to the field," she said at last. They slithered along a muddy path through the woods to a level expanse of grass which was too soggy to walk on.

"This must be where they play games," said Carrie. "It said in the brochure there's a lot of emphasis on sports. I'm not very athletic — are you?"

Eliza shook her head as she stared at the field. She was too tall and awkward to be good at games; she always tripped over her own feet. It was hard to imagine this broad, quiet space milling with students. There already seemed to be an enormous number of boarders, but tomorrow they would encounter all the day-girls as well. She glanced at Carrie. At least *one* of the many faces was becoming familiar. And a good thing about her cheerful companion was that she talked so much; all Eliza had to do was reply.

"What do you think of Helen?" Carrie asked her.

"Uhhh . . . I don't know yet." Helen was one of the many people Eliza was saving up to contemplate in bed.

"*I* think she's weird. I hate the way she stares. And last night she strung up my hippo from the light with her shoe-lace. Pam's stuck-up, and Jean's really shy. She goes into the bathroom to get undressed. I'm so glad you're here, Eliza," said Carrie for the second time that day. "I just know we're going to be good friends."

This was embarrassing. Eliza had always heard, however, that Americans were very friendly, and she glowed inside at Carrie's words. Still, she didn't know what to say in answer. She tapped the other girl on the shoulder. "Race you back!" she called.

By eight o'clock on Sunday evening Eliza felt that she'd always been at Ashdown, and that nothing in her former world existed. She sat with Carrie and Jean on Carrie's bed, as they stitched the school crest onto their berets and blazers. Helen and Pam were watching TV downstairs. Eliza studied the crest as she sewed — a single bluebell against a pale blue background, with the school motto curling around it.

She felt more confident with just the other two new girls in the dorm, even though she had barely spoken a word to Jean. Pam had enlisted the quiet girl all afternoon to help sort out her many clothes because Miss Bixley was letting her keep only a small number of them upstairs.

"Do you like that book?" Eliza asked, pointing to the one on Jean's bed.

Jean's narrow face grew animated. "Oh, yes — I love animal stories."

"I like the bull terrier in it the best," said Eliza.

"Have you — I mean — is that a picture of *your* dog on your dresser?"

"She belongs to my whole family." Eliza told Jean how Jessie had travelled from Edmonton to Toronto in a crate. Then she was silent while she wondered if Jessie had recovered from the experience. Carrie told them about her family's four cats.

"I'm not allowed to have an animal," said Jean in a small voice. "My mother thinks they're dirty."

"Well, none of us can have pets *here*," said Carrie kindly. "So we're all the same as you."

They heard Helen and Pam stomping down the hall, and glanced at one another reassuringly. Then it was Lights Out. "And not a sound," said Miss Bixley. "Sleep tight, girls."

Eliza squirmed in her bed, trying to find a place to fit between the lumps. It was a relief to lie in the dark with her own thoughts again. Exhaustion seeped from her body into the mattress.

Then something dug into her back from below, and she was lifted high into the air and slowly lowered. She yelped with alarm until she realized it was Helen underneath her, pushing up with her feet.

"Scared you, didn't I?" chuckled Helen.

"N-not really," said Eliza, trying to sound calm. "Just surprised me."

"Shhh! We'll get into trouble if we talk," whispered Pam.

"Not with Bix on duty," said Helen. "She doesn't come upstairs until late. The one to watch is the Pouncer — that's Mrs Renfrew, and she's a terror. She has us on Bix's nights off. And sometimes Charlie comes around, but not too often."

Charlie? That must be Miss Tavistock. Eliza knew her first name was Charlotte, but Charlie seemed an odd nickname for such a dignified person.

Helen finished describing the matrons. "I had Waltzing Matilda last year in the Nursery. She was always checking on us. They treat you like babies up there. But this year we should be able to get something started — especially since this dorm is so out of the way."

"Like what?" asked Eliza, her curiosity overcoming the unsettling feeling Helen gave her.

"Wait and see, Eliza Doolittle — it's not time yet."

"Be quiet," hissed Pam. "Carrie and Jean are already asleep."

Eliza was wakened by something in the middle of the night. It was the sound of muffled sobs, and it came from Jean's bed. Should she say something? She knew that if she were the one crying, she'd rather do it privately.

Finally Jean was quiet, but now Eliza felt close to tears. She groped for John, but he had fallen on the floor and she didn't want to disturb anyone by getting down to pick him up.

Pulling open the curtain beside her bed, she gazed out at the thin new moon shining down on the tennis courts. She knew it was new, not old, because her father had once told her the old moon was in the shape of a "C," which meant "contracting." She wondered if her parents could see the moon in Toronto. Then she almost did cry.

The moon looked lonely. You wanted to come here, Eliza reminded herself again, and at last she drifted again into an uneasy sleep.

III

Helen

Dear Mum and Dad,

It was wonderful to talk to you last night, but too short! Now I'll tell you all about Ashdown.

I'm in the Yellow Dorm and I have four dorm-mates. I like Carrie the best. She's from Seattle and she has five older brothers and sisters. Jean's from Chilliwack, and she goes home every Saturday. Pam's from Vancouver, and she's our dorm head. She's very bossy. Helen's from Prince George. She's always getting into trouble.

Our matron is Miss Bixley. We're lucky because she's the nicest one.

We get up every day at 7. There is a very loud bell. We have breakfast at 8, and school starts at 9 and ends at 3. Then we have games or go for a walk with the matron. We have to walk two by two in a long line! At 4:30 we change for dinner, and then we have prep for an hour (that's what the time when we do our homework is called). After dinner there's prayers, then more prep, then we go to bed at 9 o'clock.

On Saturdays we have prep in the morning, and then we can go out until 8 and don't have to go to bed until 9:30. Carrie came out with me this Saturday and Uncle Adrian took us to Stanley Park.

The food isn't bad, except for Tuesdays. It is going to be the same every week.

Monday — Shepherd's Pie
Tuesday — Liver and Onions (yuck!)
Wednesday — Chicken
Thursday — Stew
Friday — Fish
Sunday — a roast at noon (but it's called
        Sunday dinner) and eggs at night

My homeroom teacher is Miss Clark, and she also teaches us English. She's very pretty. I am in 7A and so is Pam. Carrie, Helen, and Jean are in 7B. It's not too hard, except for French. They start it earlier here.

My piano teacher, Mrs Fraser, is really good — she makes me work harder than the one in Edmonton though. I get to miss part of prep to practise, and I also practise before breakfast every day.

Miss Tavistock is strict, but I like her. She calls me Elizabeth. So do all the teachers, but the matrons call me Eliza.

Next Saturday all the boarders are going on a picnic to Saltspring Island.

Please make sure Jessie gets brushed every day. I'm so glad she's not trying to run away. Give the Demons a kiss for me. Please send me some of those cookies with the nuts and raisins in them. Would a cake crumble in the mail? We're allowed to keep our own food downstairs.

I miss you very much, but I'm happy here. It's just like I thought it would be.

                              With heaps of love,
XOXOXOXOXO   Eliza

P.S.   Please send me a flashlight.

There! Eliza shook out her aching hand and stretched full length on her bed. It felt good to write everything down in a letter. And her parents had sounded so worried on the phone, she had to assure them she was all right.

She *was,* although she felt more bewildered by everything than she would have admitted to them. So much had been crowded into this long first week — so many new faces and new voices and new subjects and new rules — that it was difficult to sort it out. But she liked the way the days ran so smoothly, with a slot for each activity. There were fascinating people to watch, and most of them were friendly. Already she knew the names of all the junior and intermediate boarders in the Old Residence. She *did* like it here — almost as much as she'd written.

She wrote another letter to one of her friends in Edmonton, telling her the same things. Maggie, however, would probably not be interested; she had just sent a long epistle filled with dull details about a boy she liked. Already Eliza felt so immersed in her new life that her friend seemed like a stranger.

She glanced around the Yellow Dorm. It was Sunday rest time, and no one dared say a word: the Pouncer was on duty. Carrie and Jean were reading. Pam was winding white tape around her grass hockey stick. Eliza had played hockey twice herself this week. All she'd done was to chug up and down the field, purposely avoiding coming near the ball. A lot of the other players appeared to be doing the same, but no one noticed.

She wondered what Helen, unusually still, was up to underneath her. The only really uncomfortable part of school so far was Helen. The volatile girl both alarmed and intrigued her. She was prickly and funny at the same time, and the liveliest person in the Old Residence.

All of the Yellow Dorm liked food, but Helen ate more than any of them. She won the toast-eating contests at her table every morning. "I don't mean to be personal," Pam told her, "but you should go on a diet."

"And you should mind your own business," retorted Helen.

The two of them were always scrapping. "When I found out I had to board, I was hoping Helen would be in the other grade seven dorm," Pam confided to Eliza and Carrie. "Last year she came to a barbeque I had

for the whole class, and she started everyone making
water bombs in the swimming pool out of paper cups.
My mother says she's a disruptive influence." Pam
tried to tell them more about all the trouble Helen
had caused in grade six, but Eliza and Carrie didn't
like her righteous tone and changed the subject.

Helen never missed an opportunity of needling
Pam, but she was fairly pleasant to the rest of them.
As well as calling Pam and Eliza "P.J." and "Eliza Doo-
little," she had nicknames for the others. Jean was
"Scotty," and Carrie was "Turps," after a ball bounc-
ing rhyme the juniors were always chanting:

Queen, Queen Caroline
Washed her hair in turpentine
Turpentine made it shine
Queen, Queen Caroline.

Already Helen had had to "go and speak to Miss
Tavistock," a threat the matrons were always holding
over them. On Tuesday evening Jean had locked herself in the bathroom when the wobbly old doorknobs
had fallen off. The rest of them heard her timid knocks
and cries, growing louder as she became more frightened. They crowded around the door.

"I'll go and get a matron," said Pam quickly.

"No — wait!" Helen looked overjoyed that something was happening. "They'll just make a fuss. Keep
calm, Scotty," she called. "We're going to rescue you!
Come on, everyone — push!"

She thrust her weight against the door and

pounded it rhythmically. The flimsy panel showed a crack of light at each shove.

The others watched her doubtfully. "Wouldn't it be better to try to get the doorknobs back on?" suggested Eliza.

"*Stop* it, Helen — you're going to break it!" cried Pam.

"That's . . . the . . . idea!" puffed Helen, red in the face. The door crashed inwards with a screech of ripping wood. Helen fell in with it. Jean screamed, then laughed nervously as she realized she was free.

In an instant both Miss Bixley and Miss Monaghan were there, gazing in disbelief at the shards of wood hanging from the side of the door.

When Helen returned from seeing Miss Tavistock, she wouldn't tell them what the headmistress had said. But her ecstatic mood had disappeared. "Everyone blames me for everything around here," she growled. "I was only trying to help." Underneath the grumbling, however, she seemed secretly triumphant.

Eliza wasn't sure where she stood with Helen. When the other girl used her nickname she felt they were on friendly terms; at other times the two of them were uneasy with each other.

Her feelings were especially mixed on Thursday. In the morning Eliza and Helen were alone in the dorm; they were the last to change their sheets. Eliza found it tricky to do this on an upper bunk, especially when the bed was so close to the wall. Helen hadn't even started. Her clean sheets were folded on her chair and she sprawled across her stripped mattress, reading

a Batman comic. Every so often she peered at Eliza
moving around her. She looked superior, as if she,
Helen, did not have to bother with such a dreary task.

It made Eliza nervous, being alone with her.
Neither of them spoke. The silence made Eliza even
more jittery, and she flapped her top sheet to make a
noise. It knocked John off her bed — and out of the
open window.

She ran to it, leaned out and spied him on the
ground below. He had landed on his back and, with
his paws spread out, looked as if he were appealing
for help.

"What are you doing, Eliza Doolittle?" yawned
Helen, throwing her comic onto the floor.

"My bear's fallen out!" Eliza started to leave the
room.

Helen stopped her. "Why don't you just go down
the fire escape?" The wooden structure went all the
way up their side of the residence, past the window by
Carrie's bed. Eliza examined it and saw that it would be
a lot faster than going around the building. She opened
the window wider, stepped onto the stairs, dashed
down and snatched up John, then scurried up again.

But after breakfast Miss Tavistock said to her
quietly, "Would you please see me in my study,
Elizabeth?"

It was strictly forbidden to go on the fire escape,
the headmistress told her firmly, after she had closed
the door. Mrs Renfrew had spotted Eliza from her
room in the New Residence and reported her.

"I'm s-sorry, Miss Tavistock," said Eliza, standing

in front of the desk and trying not to cry. How terrible to do something wrong her very first week! "I didn't know it wasn't allowed — I just went to get my bear." Admitting that she had a bear sounded so babyish that her cheeks flamed.

Miss Tavistock's voice softened. "If you didn't know, Elizabeth, then I forgive you. I know you're not the type of girl to intentionally break a rule, and it's hard to remember everything at first." The head-mistress raised her eyebrows. "But goodness me, your dormitory is troublesome this week! I hope this isn't an indication of how you're all going to behave for the rest of the year!"

"I'm sorry, Eliza Doolittle," said Helen nonchalantly when Eliza confronted her later. "I thought you *knew* it wasn't allowed, and I didn't think you'd get caught."

Eliza wondered if she should believe her. Getting into trouble seemed unimportant to Helen, and she did appear genuinely amazed that Eliza was upset about it. It would be safest, however, not to trust the other girl.

But that night she changed her mind again. Eliza had quickly discovered she was the only one in the Yellow Dorm who still wore an undershirt. No one except Pam seemed to need a bra, but each person wore one as if it were a badge of membership in grade seven. Eliza had no wish to acquire something so grown-up, but she also hoped the others wouldn't comment on her difference. So far, they hadn't.

On that Thursday evening, however, Pam examined Eliza thoughtfully as they were undressing.

"Don't you think you should ask Miss Bixley to get you a bra, Eliza? You can get padded ones," she added sweetly.

Eliza's face burned. She turned her back on Pam to hide both her flat chest and her sudden tears.

But now she was facing Helen, who had been standing behind her. The red-haired girl looked straight at Eliza; even behind her glasses, her sympathy was apparent. Then her eyes shifted to Pam and glinted with fury.

"You leave Eliza alone, P.J.!" she hissed. "It's none of your business if she wears a bra or not. I hate mine. My mother only got it because it was an option on the clothing list this year. In fact, I think I'll get rid of it." She picked up the white cotton garment and twirled it around her head dramatically. Then she flung it into the wastepaper basket.

Pam looked offended. "I was only trying to give Eliza some advice, Helen. Don't get so excited."

Eliza finished buttoning up her pyjama top. She blinked back her tears and smiled at Helen. "Thanks," she mouthed. Helen actually winked at her.

The next morning Miss Bixley found the bra and made Helen take it back, but Eliza couldn't forget her surprising defence.

"Time to go down to the dining room and write your letters home, girls." Mrs Renfrew's no-nonsense Scottish voice pierced the Sunday silence. She crept about so quietly, she always surprised them.

"I've done mine," said Eliza, slipping her second letter into an envelope and addressing it.

"So've I," said Helen, emerging from underneath with a small grubby envelope.

The Pouncer looked suspicious, but took the letters to mail. "Very well, you two may begin your free time, but I want you to stay inside. It's too wet to go out. The rest of you hurry up, please."

"Mrs Renfrew, I can't find my green sweater," complained Carrie, all her dresser drawers gaping.

"I found it under your bed this morning, Carrie," said the Pouncer. "It's in the Pound. You'll have to pay me a dime to get it out." She sniffed disapprovingly. "We're going to make a lot of money out of *this* dormitory, I can see that already."

Eliza shoved her writing paper quickly into a drawer. The only tidy person in the dorm was Pam. She was so extreme she made up for the rest of them, draping her pristine uniform carefully over a chair each night in readiness for the next morning.

When Carrie, Jean and Pam had left, Eliza got out a book and prepared to sink into it. One problem with boarding school so far was that there wasn't enough time to read. Settling back against her pillow, she was immediately transported into Roman Britain.

But Helen's voice underneath her broke the spell. "Listen, Eliza. It's time to make plans."

"Plans?" asked Eliza, reluctantly putting down *The Eagle of the Ninth*.

Helen moved across to Pam's bed. She fixed her glasses on Eliza as if they were a pair of binoculars.

"Yes. It's a plan for all of us, but I wanted to tell you first. You seem to be gutsier than the others. I liked the way you rescued your silly bear, even if you didn't know you were breaking a rule. Will you support me if I suggest something to everyone?"

Eliza felt flattered and frightened at the same time. She didn't want Helen to look down on her, but she didn't want to clash with Miss Tavistock again either.

"It depends what it is," she said as agreeably as she could. But Helen looked ruffled.

"Oh, don't bother if you're worried about it. I guess you *are* just as chicken as the rest of them."

Eliza was ashamed. After all, in her books the boarders were always planning some prank or another. Wasn't that one reason she'd wanted to come here — for excitement? She had never thought of herself as a coward, and she wondered why she felt afraid.

"I'll support you," she said quickly. "Tell me what it is."

IV

A Long Feast

"Eliza and I have an idea," Helen announced that night. By now they chattered fearlessly for an extended period after Lights Out — except when the Pouncer was on duty.

Eliza clutched John under the covers. She was just as curious as the others, for Helen had told her only part of the plan.

"What we propose," said Helen, getting out of bed, opening the curtains and squatting on the floor so she could see them all, "is a game. A Daring Game. This place is boring. We need to do something to liven it up."

"I don't think it's boring," protested Carrie. Eliza agreed silently; everything was too new to be boring. But she liked games. She and Maggie and some other friends in Edmonton used to play at being knights, or

Robin Hood, or horses, until the others told her they were too old.

This game sounded different — not pretending, but real, which made it riskier. It had the same allure of important secrecy, however, that had been present in her other games. Helen's bravado when she described it had a lot to do with this. Eliza had never known anyone her own age who seemed so sure of herself.

Remembering her role, she made her voice sound enthusiastic: "It might be fun." She watched Carrie listen to Helen with more interest.

Pam lay on her back and stared at the ceiling. "Well, go on, Helen. But I won't play if it's dangerous or anything."

Jean, silent as usual, just watched Helen with wide eyes.

Helen grinned at Eliza, who felt relieved she'd said the right thing.

"Okay," continued Helen, "a Daring Game. What we'll do is take turns doing dares. I can think of lots, but you can make up some too, if you want. It has to be something that takes a lot of nerve."

"But what's the point?" said Pam.

"The point is to do it, of course. It'll be fun to see how much we can get away with in this dump."

That was a mistake. Pam rolled over. "Well, count me out. I don't want to get into trouble, and I'm the dorm head, so I don't think any of you should do it."

So far, thought Eliza, the job of being dorm head

consisted of informing everyone of the position; its only duty seemed to be the collection of the laundry slips each week.

"You haven't even heard what the first dare is," said Helen. "You'll like it, I bet. It's for all of us." Pam refused to answer, but the others begged her to continue.

"A dorm feast. I dare us all to bring food up here this Saturday and have a huge feast after Lights Out."

Eliza stretched out her legs with relief. She'd imagined all sorts of dreadful things Helen might have proposed. Dorm feasts, however, seemed a requirement of boarding school. She was surprised at the tameness of the first dare, but she decided that Helen probably wanted to test them with an easy one.

"Come on, Pam, how about it?" said Helen, in an unusually wheedling tone. "Everyone has feasts. The Red Dorm had one last week. We had three when I was in the Nursery, and we never got caught."

"I have some chocolate bars in my tuck box," said Carrie.

"Maybe my aunt would make us a cake," said Eliza.

"I think I could bring something from home," said Jean softly. They waited for Pam to reply.

"Oh, all right," she said finally. "If everyone else does it I suppose it's okay. As long as you're sure we won't get caught. I'm going out with Deb this Saturday — I'll get some buns or something."

"Let's make a list!" Carrie jumped out of bed to find a paper and pencil.

By nine-thirty on Saturday night, the food that had been concealed beneath coats, hurried up the stairs and stashed under beds, in drawers and in the closet far exceeded the items on the list.

"Goodnight, girls," said Miss Bixley, turning out the light. They waited fifteen minutes, then arranged all the food in the middle of the floor on Pam's large bath towel. Drawing back the curtains, they sat cross-legged in a circle around the feast, gazing at its beauty with relish.

A glistening pile of red licorice sticks
A box of Stoned Wheat Thins
A jar of peanut butter
Three American chocolate bars
A giant bottle of Coke
Half a dozen Bismarck doughnuts, oozing with jam
One slightly squashed chocolate cake
Six pieces of fried chicken

"Who bought all the licorice?" asked Carrie.

"I did," said Helen. "When Bix took us for our walk yesterday I persuaded her to let us stop at Crabby Crump's."

They all preferred the twisting red licorice sticks from Crump's Groceries across the street to any other kind. Mrs Crump disliked the noisy Ashdown girls who crowded her tiny store, but they gave her so much business she had to put up with them.

"I thought you said you had to spend all your pocket money on buying a new math scribbler," said Pam nastily. They all knew Helen had dropped her old scribbler in a mud puddle on purpose because she hadn't done her homework.

Helen shrugged. "Oh, I had some left over." The two dollars they collected in small brown envelopes from the office every Friday never went very far. Much of the food for the feast was donated from the downstairs tuck boxes that were kept full with "care packages" from parents. Helen, however, was never sent anything from home.

Pam looked as if she didn't believe Helen, but she became distracted by the chocolate bars Carrie was cutting into five pieces each with her nail file. "Yum," munched Pam, biting into part of an Almond Joy. "I've always wanted to know what these taste like."

Carrie dipped her piece into some peanut butter. "Try it this way — it's tremendous."

"They should feed us like this all the time instead of starving us," said Helen, holding a piece of chicken in one hand and a doughnut in the other, taking alternate bites of each. She hummed the song they had learned on the picnic last week, and they started singing it softly, the words muffled by food and laughter.

There is a boarding school
Far, far away
Where they get onion soup
Three times a day.
Oh, how those boarders yell
When they hear the dinner bell!
Oh, how those onions smell
Three times a day!

Jean chewed licorice cheerfully; bits of it stuck to the wires in her mouth and she picked them off. "I hate braces," she whispered to Eliza beside her. Jean had stopped crying at night, but she still looked like a scared rabbit most of the time. Tonight, however, she was a little more relaxed.

Pam was spreading the crackers evenly with peanut butter, using the round end of her toothbrush. She paused. "Do you hear something?" They listened hard, but there wasn't a sound; the whole house of boarders was asleep.

"It's just your imagination, P.J.," said Helen. "Bix won't come up for ages."

The lights from the parking lot created eerie squares of light across the wall and ceiling. Eliza shuffled closer into the circle. For the first time she felt as if they were a real group instead of five separate personalities. Almost like a family of five sisters, even though sisters wouldn't be so different from one another. It was more like a pyjama party that never ended, with no parents to tell you to go to sleep. For a second this thought made Eliza lonely. Then it made her feel curiously free.

At home there were two people who knew her intimately and always had her welfare in mind — her parents. Here there was much more outward authority, but there were too many students for anyone in charge to be able to know the inner state of any one girl. Her outside — what she wore, where she was at different times of the day, what activities she did at those times — was much more strictly controlled here than it was at home. But it was exhilarating to realize that no one was responsible for her inside but herself.

Eliza raised her toothbrush glass full of Coke. "Here's to the Yellow Dorm," she whispered. The others joined her in a silent toast.

Ten minutes later none of them could get down another morsel, but there was still a lot of food piled on the towel.

Helen thrust a drumstick at Eliza. "Have another piece of chicken."

"Ohhh, I can't," groaned Eliza, who had already had a large dinner at her aunt and uncle's.

"We'll have to put it away and sneak it into our tuck boxes tomorrow," said Pam. They gathered the food up quickly into a paper bag and stowed it in the closet. Then they staggered back to bed.

"That was the best feast I've ever had," sighed Helen. "I think you all performed our first dare very well. I am extremely proud of you, girls," she added, imitating Miss Tavistock.

She had barely finished her sentence when the lights flashed on, and a voice said crisply, "What is going on in here?"

It wasn't Miss Bixley. It was Miss Tavistock.

"N-nothing, Miss Tavistock," stammered Pam.

"I can smell chicken. Do you have food in the dormitory? You know that is forbidden."

There was no use concealing it. No one ever dared hide anything from Miss Tavistock. Morosely, Helen pulled the paper bag out of the closet.

The headmistress peered into its greasy depths, wrinkling her nose with distaste. "Very well. Put on your dressing-gowns and slippers and come downstairs. Bring the food with you."

Eliza climbed down and nervously jerked her dressing-gown sleeve over the flannelette sleeve of her pyjamas. Her knees shook with an almost pleasant kind of fear. What was going to happen to them? This was probably a greater crime than going onto the fire escape by accident, but she was more curious than frightened. And this time they were all in trouble together.

Carrie seemed to feel the same. All the way down the stairs she squeezed Eliza's arm. "Oooh, I'm so scared," she breathed, but she sounded as if she were going to laugh.

"Silence, please," said Miss Tavistock. She led them along the dark hall into the dining room and made them sit on both sides of one of the long tables.

"Put everything on the table, Helen," she ordered. "Pamela, fetch some plates from the kitchen. Since you seem to be so hungry for extra food, you can finish your meal down here."

They looked at one another with horror. Finish it! Eliza's stomach lurched in protest as she stared at the mess Helen was spreading out on the table. The remains of the chocolate bars were stuck to the chicken. Squashed doughnuts leaked their fillings onto broken crackers. The empty Coke bottle was smeared with chocolate icing, and the cake had disintegrated into soggy crumbs. Pam's toothbrush, encrusted with dried peanut butter, lay ludicrously on top of it all.

"Oh, please, Miss Tavistock, I *can't* eat any more!" begged Carrie.

"We won't do it again, Miss Tavistock. I'll be sick if I have another bite!" said Pam.

"No arguing. Eat it up, every crumb. Come along, Elizabeth, have another piece of chicken. Helen, you're the one who's starving — have some licorice."

She heard us, thought Eliza, turning a minuscule piece of chicken around and around in her mouth. But she waited until we'd finished. She looked at Miss Tavistock sitting erectly at the head of the table. The headmistress always wore tailored suits. Tonight it was her plainest black one, but the white blouse underneath had just a hint of ruffle at the neck. Eliza thought for a second she was trying not to smile.

She liked the headmistress more all the time. The old girls warned the new girls not to get on the wrong side of her. But Eliza couldn't imagine Miss Tavistock ever being really mean or unfair, the way some of the headmistresses in her books were.

Her awe of Miss Tavistock had lessened last week when the headmistress had shown her and Carrie her stamp collection. Eliza had received a letter from her English grandmother, and Miss Tavistock had stopped them in the hall after prayers one evening and asked if she could have the stamp.

"I especially like British ones," she said, smiling. "Come and see my collection." Out of one of her desk drawers she pulled a bulging album crammed with tiny squares of colour, like hundreds of miniature paintings. Her voice grew animated as she talked about them. Carrie said afterwards she thought the explanation would never stop. Eliza found it interesting, however, and resolved to ask for a stamp album for Christmas.

Thinking about Miss Tavistock was not making eating any easier. The only sound was the low ticking of the clock down the hall and five mouths chewing hesitantly. No one, not even Helen, could force down more than a few mouthfuls, and Jean looked pale.

"All right, girls," said Miss Tavistock finally. "I think you've learned your lesson. Throw it all away and then you can sit in the hall for fifteen minutes. I hope I will never catch you with food in the dormitory again."

Sitting in the hall without speaking was a common punishment. The headmistress arranged them on chairs down its length, then went into her study. Eliza was sitting under the clock. Its steady voice was reassuring in the darkness.

Miss Bixley came out of the matrons' sitting room, noticed her five charges and stopped in astonishment, then wagged her finger at them and continued up the stairs.

Despite never wanting to eat again, Eliza felt peaceful for the first time since she'd come to Ashdown. This was what boarding school was supposed to be like, getting into trouble with your dorm-mates and feeling a bond of companionship with them because of it. She glanced over her shoulder cautiously and grinned at Carrie.

When they were all back in bed, Pam risked a whisper. "I don't like your game, Helen. I'm not going to play it ever again."

But Eliza burrowed contentedly into her pillow. At least we've proved to Helen we're not cowards, she thought as she fell asleep.

V

Being Good

Helen said no more about dares for the next month, and Eliza had enough to do without them. Her life was now divided into three distinct areas: the residence, the school and Saturdays. The school part was the most intense and overwhelmed everything else. Eliza was relieved to break from its whirl of activity each day to the quieter atmosphere of the residence, where she now felt very much at home. She was just as glad to have a rest from the dorm at her aunt and uncle's every Saturday.

The boarders made up only a fifth of the student population of Ashdown, but sometimes Eliza couldn't resist thinking they were superior to the rest. One rule, as cooler weather approached, was that everyone had to wear her coat going between buildings. Everyone except the boarders, who wore capes instead — navy-blue gabardine lined in grey, with pointed hoods. Eliza flung the folds of her cape dramatically around her each morning before she crossed the strip of concrete that separated the residence from the school. Sometimes she pretended she was one of the Three Musketeers. As she filed into prayers she savoured the importance of standing out as a caped boarder.

She had become friendly with only one of the day-girls, Thea Crawford, an inquisitive girl who pumped her for every detail of boarding. The dorm feast had enthralled her. It made a good long story.

Many of the other day-girls, however, seemed to look down on the boarders. Even though they travelled to Ashdown from different parts of the city, they all appeared to know each other outside of school. Their confident talk of yacht clubs and horseback riding and ski chalets made Eliza feel excluded.

Pam hung around with the day-girls as if she were still one herself. She was the only member of the Yellow Dorm in Eliza's class, but she almost ignored Eliza in school hours. And Pam was the sole boarder admitted into the top level of the three-part hierarchy in 7A: winners, losers and in-betweeners. Eliza was used to being an in-betweener; she had been one in her last school. But she was insulted when one day-girl asked her: "Why were you sent away to school? Were you a problem at home?"

Most of the school's activities centred on the six houses it was divided into, all named after trees. Eliza was in Cedar. Everyone was knitting squares to join together into afghans for the Red Cross, and Cedar had the most so far. Eliza, Carrie, Jean and Pam often sat up with the curtains open after Lights Out, knitting furiously.

Carrie was the fastest. "You should see my grandmother," she boasted. "She doesn't even have to look at the needles. She used to win prizes in Norway." Jean knit almost as rapidly as Carrie. Eliza was slower, but she worked at it so steadily that she had completed more squares than any of them.

Pam was a beginner and hadn't even got through one square yet. "I never learned," she said. She watched Carrie's nimble fingers enviously, for she was just as keen as Eliza to win points for her house.

"Didn't your mother teach you?" asked Eliza. She remembered the rainy Saturday four years earlier when her mother had shown her how to knit a scarf for John.

Pam flushed. "She never had time. The housekeeper tried to once, but she gave up when I kept dropping stitches."

Jean took Pam's square from her to correct a mistake. "Do you really have a housekeeper?"

"We did before my parents moved. She's still in our house, working for the people who rented it."

"We have a cook," said Carrie. "But that's because my mother manages our store all day."

Eliza was fascinated. She'd never known anyone with servants before. Pam and Carrie must be as rich as some of the day-girls. You could tell by their clothes, and all the places they had been, that their families had more money than Jean's, Helen's and her own.

It occurred to her that Pam used Jean as a servant. She was always getting Jean to make sure the soap was out of her hair when she rinsed it, or to time her crawl when they went swimming at the Empire Pool. In the residence the two of them were becoming a pair, just as she and Carrie were. It surprised her that Jean would put up with Pam's bossiness. But the timid girl seemed grateful to have such an authoritative person to hide behind.

Helen didn't knit. She was subdued these days, and Eliza wondered what she was plotting. Most of her free time she spent listening to her new radio.

"How can you afford that?" Pam had asked when Helen had brought it in the week before. Pam had the only other radio in the dorm.

"Oh, my mother sent me some money," said Helen vaguely.

Pam assumed her most priggish expression. "You're supposed to put extra money in the office. I could report you, you know."

They knew she wouldn't. Helen just gave her a withering look, to show what she thought of tattle-tales.

One evening Eliza sat in one of the music rooms in the gym, finishing another square and trying to read the last chapter of her book at the same time. She was supposed to be practising, but there was still time to finish the square and play a piece or two before she had to go. Pushing the last stitch off the needle, she snipped the yellow wool, poked its end through the loop and drew it tight — there, one more done. It wasn't quite a square, but she could stretch it. Reading would have to wait until later. She opened up her Grade V Royal Conservatory of Music of Toronto book to her List A piece, Little Prelude No. 2. The notes flooded into one another as she pressed the loud pedal guiltily. She knew that if Mrs Fraser were listening she would tell her not to overdo it.

Scales could be skipped today; they needed practice, but there were three days left until her next lesson. She went on to her hymn. This week Eliza was going to play the hymn at evening prayers for the first time. It was an easy one and she already knew it well, but she wanted to get it absolutely right.

One of her favourite rituals at Ashdown was the singing of hymns. There were three a day, two in the morning and one at night. Eliza liked to make her voice sound exalted in lines like "Early in the mor-r-r-rning, our song shall rise to thee." Once Helen, standing behind her in 7B, jabbed her and hissed that she sang too loudly. Eliza didn't care. She knew her voice was only average, but she could carry a tune. When she sang alone she sounded weak, but in a group she could let her voice soar freely, as if it belonged to someone else. There had never been enough singing in public school to satisfy her. Here there was choir as well as prayers, and sometimes there were hootenannies on Sunday evenings.

Someone was playing the piano next door, and the melody was so compelling that she stopped and listened. Three notes, over and over, changing slightly

every few phrases. The bass chords chimed in softly,
then a treble section picked out a hesitant melody. The
melancholy strains suited the October dusk outside the
window. She crept to the open door of the next room
to hear better.

It was Madeline; she should have known. Madeline Wood was the best pianist in the whole school. A
grade eleven boarder, she was also Cedar's house captain. Eliza admired her so much she could barely
speak to her. She saw Madeline only on house meeting days, or at a distance in the dining room and in
prayers. But she always kept an eye out for her long
dark hair and the slash of green ribbon she wore across
her sweater as an emblem of her office.

Each of them in the Yellow Dorm, except Helen,
had a special favourite among the older girls. Pam and
Jean were part of a bevy of grade sevens who clustered
around the head girl, Laura Singer, every break, trying
to win her attention. Carrie liked Julie Cassidy, a
prefect and fellow American who knew Carrie's sisters
in Seattle.

But Eliza preferred Madeline. The older girl was
tiny, but she had an air of quiet authority, and her
eyes always looked amused. Every time Eliza handed
her another square, Madeline would say, "Good for
you, Eliza! What a hard worker you are!"

Now Eliza listened to the last notes of the dream-
like melody. There was a yearning quality to the music, and it made her ache for something that seemed
just out of reach. The final chord was so hushed it

almost didn't exist. Then Madeline sat perfectly still, as if in a trance.

Eliza felt like an eavesdropper. She couldn't just tiptoe away and not say anything. "That was wonderful," she breathed. "What's it called?"

Madeline swung around on the piano stool. "Oh, it's you, Eliza! That's the *Moonlight* Sonata. I'm trying to get it ready for a recital, but I have a long way to go."

"Oh no — it's perfect."

"Thank you!" Madeline sounded as if Eliza's opinion really counted. She glanced at her watch. "I've finished for today. How about you? Did you have a good practice? I heard your Bach."

Eliza blushed to think how much of the half-hour she'd wasted on other activities. She felt proud, however, that Madeline was speaking to her as a fellow pianist. "I think I use too much loud pedal," she mumbled, "but it's hard not to."

She came in and sat on the windowsill, and they discussed the use of the pedals like two professionals. It was the longest she had ever talked to Madeline, and she chose her words carefully. Madeline listened so attentively that she made Eliza want to be her best self.

"How do you like boarding so far?" the older girl asked her. "Do you miss your parents?"

"I don't really have time to," Eliza confessed.

Madeline's green eyes crinkled into slits. "Well, they certainly keep us busy here. You seem to be fitting in all right."

Miss Tavistock had said the same thing last week: "I'm very pleased with you, Elizabeth. You're doing well in your work and really taking part in the life of the school."

"I like it here," Eliza told Madeline. She meant it. It had seemed odd to be away from Ashdown for three whole days during the Thanksgiving weekend at her aunt and uncle's. She had been impatient to get back. The perfect weather added to her satisfaction. It wasn't like a prairie fall, where the wind whipped the branches bare of leaves as quickly as they turned yellow. Here the trees changed slowly, gradually ripening into golds and reds.

"Do *you* like it?" asked Eliza. "How old were you when you came?"

"I came in grade nine. I like it well enough, and Mrs Fraser's one of the best piano teachers in the province. But sometimes I get tired of it. I'm glad I only have a year to go."

Eliza was shocked. "Tired of it! I'll never get tired of it!"

"You're certainly enthusiastic," laughed Madeline. "And it's great to have you in my house. Look at all the house points you've earned for us already!"

The bell clanged insistently from the Old Residence. "Prep's over," said Madeline. "Let's go to dinner."

They walked out of the gym together. The tree trunks by the driveway were black shadows against the dim sky. Eliza shivered, partly because of the crisp

air, but mostly because of the pleasure of being with
Madeline.

Two evenings later Eliza sat at the piano at the back of
the Blue Sitting Room, her knees shaking, her hands
wet and her eyes fixed on Miss Tavistock standing in
front of the assembled boarders.

"Hymn 636."

This would be the worst part: playing one verse
alone so everyone would learn the melody. Her hands
slipped and trembled on the keys, and she whispered
the words to herself to keep time.

> *Work,* for the *night* is *com*ing!
> *Work* through the *mor*ning *hours*

She pounded the keys hard and began to relax. By the
time the singers all opened their mouths she was in
full swing, throwing herself into the melody, playing
faster and faster, driven by the force of their voices
behind her notes.

> *Give* every *fly*ing *mi*-i-nute
> *Some*thing to *keep* in *store*

"Slow down, Eliza!" someone whispered in her
ear. She tried to, but the rhythm was too infectious.
Drawing out the last line as Mrs Fraser had taught her,
however, she finished with a resounding "Amen." Her
hands dropped to her lap; she was panting.

Miss Tavistock smiled. "Thank you, Elizabeth."

After prayers Helen cornered Eliza as the rest of the boarders milled about the room before returning to prep. "Why did you choose *that* hymn? Are you trying to give us a hint?"

"What do you mean?"

"It sounds like you're telling us to study," grumbled Helen. Carrie had told Eliza that Mrs Fitch, the 7B teacher, was always accusing Helen of being lazy.

"I don't think it means *that*," said Eliza. "I didn't mean it to, anyhow. I picked it because it's one of the easiest in the book."

"Listen, Eliza," said Helen, with one of her owlish stares. "I've been meaning to tell you something. You're getting far too sucky."

"Sucky?"

"Yes. You know — sucking up to Charlie and Madeline and the rest of them. Playing hymns, knitting squares, studying all the time. You're turning into a goody-goody. When we started the Daring Game I thought you had guts, but now you're acting like Pam."

Eliza felt a familiar stabbing pain. At her last school she had sometimes been accused of being a teacher's pet. It seemed unfair. Adults were often pleased with her, but that wasn't her fault. She liked having their approval, but she didn't deliberately try for it as Pam did. Her parents had often told her how sensible she was for her age. Once she'd even overheard her Toronto grandmother saying she was "delightfully old-fashioned." Eliza had cringed at this image of herself. But she couldn't help it if what she liked was often what older people liked.

Helen was waiting for an answer. Eliza tried not to flinch from her accusing look and held her chin high so the tears wouldn't fall from her eyes.

"I don't mean to," she said at last. "Really I don't. And I'm not like Pam at all," she added firmly.

Helen shrugged as if she didn't believe her and looked even more disdainful. Before she left the room she said, "I think it's time for another dare. Then we'll see."

VI

The Second Dare

Eliza tried to forget about Helen's accusation, but she could think of nothing else as she tossed in bed that night.

You can't help being yourself, said a voice in her head. It was her mother's, sensible and soothing as always.

But Helen doesn't like that self, Eliza answered.

Then forget about her. If she can't accept you as you are, she's not worth having as a friend. Besides, you have Carrie — you don't need Helen.

I do! thought Eliza. But she didn't know why.

Helen was overbearing and not always very nice, not the type of person Eliza usually chose for a friend. There was no reason she had to put up with someone who called her names.

Perhaps, however, the name fit. Perhaps she *was* a goody-goody. She felt angry at Helen for making her contemplate that. Maybe she *should* stay away from her. But it was unfair to dismiss Helen completely, when there was so much about her she didn't know yet. Perhaps that was why Eliza was so drawn to her: she was mysterious. And Eliza couldn't forget how Helen had stood up for her against Pam. That night, she had seemed like a real friend.

Eliza couldn't work it out. All the contentment she had felt in the last month was spoiled. It was as if Helen had taken a pin and pricked a balloon inside of her.

After that she began to avoid direct encounters with the other girl. Helen hardly spoke to Eliza either, and when she did, she didn't call her "Eliza Doolittle."

The strain between them wasn't noticed by the others, for the whole school was gripped by the frenzy of mid-term exams. No one in the Yellow Dorm had written real exams before. Pam crept out every morning at six-thirty to cram in the library. Jean carried her English book with her everywhere, whispering the poems they had to memorize. Eliza was especially worried about French and science. She listed conjugations of French verbs on scraps of paper, on her music books and on napkins. Constantly she repeated to herself the sentence Mrs Lewis, the science teacher, had taught them: "Man Very Early Made Jars Stand Up Nearly Perfect." The first letter of each word stood for a planet, and the words were in order of the planets' distances from the sun.

The only two who didn't study extra hours were Carrie and Helen. The former said to Eliza complacently, "I've done my best so far. I'm not going to worry about it." Helen just lay on her bed, cut off from the rest of them by her radio earplug, and scowled.

"Fidget's always picking on her," Carrie told Eliza. "I think it's mean. Helen fools around a lot, of course, and her work's always sloppy. But other people are like that too. She says awful things to Helen."

"Like what?"

"Well, today was the worst. Fidget came in and caught Helen and Linda O. standing on top of the desks — they were just trying to close the windows. She didn't even tell off Linda, but she yelled at Helen and said no wonder her parents sent her away to school so young — she was such a brat they must have been glad to get rid of her."

"But that's terrible! Helen should tell Miss Tavistock."

"It didn't seem to bother her. I don't think anything does. She just laughed really loud, and Fidget took off a house point for rudeness. She was the one who was rude! Some of us thought Helen should tell, but she said to forget about it. And a few kids thought she deserved it. A lot of the day-girls don't like Helen."

It must have bothered her, thought Eliza. Perhaps Mrs Fitch's bullying was what had made Helen so withdrawn lately. And why *had* Helen been sent here so young? She had never told them.

"What do *you* think of Helen?" said Eliza, remembering Carrie asking her the same question on their first day.

Carrie shrugged. "Oh, well . . . Helen's just Helen. She's not so bad." Eliza wished she could be as untroubled as Carrie was by their complicated dorm-mate.

Exam week was appropriately grey and wet. Every morning they shuffled through sodden heaps of leaves, as they trooped over to the gym for prayers. Many of the trees were bare now, although Eliza's favourite arbutus and the laurel and holly bushes around the Old Residence were still as green as new paint.

Eliza felt purged when exams were over. Each of the seven times she'd confronted the typed list of questions and the blank book to be filled with answers she had panicked. But then she'd taken a deep breath and scribbled down what she knew as carefully as she could. She thought she had done all right, even in French.

The Friday after exam week the boarders were being taken to the Queen Elizabeth Theatre to see a performance of the National Ballet. Eliza had never seen a ballet before, and that morning she tore open her folded blouse eagerly. Every week their blouses arrived back from the cleaners compressed into a starched rectangle. She popped open the sleeves and pulled the folds straight with a satisfying ripping sound.

Miss Bixley was braiding Carrie's hair. "What a lucky girl you are," she said. "I had lovely hair as a child, you know. I could sit on it, it was so long."

"It sounds like a lot of trouble to me," said Helen.

The matron was always telling them about her childhood in New York City, where she had gone briefly on the stage. This was hard to believe, but she had scrapbooks of pictures to prove it.

"Tonight we're going to play the Daring Game," Helen told them when Miss Bixley had left the room.

"But we're going out!" said Carrie.

"All the better. We'll go to bed later than usual and everyone will expect us to nod off quickly like sleepy little children."

Jean look scared. "Is the dare for all of us again?"

"No, I think we should draw names. Then I'll decide what the person who's picked has to do. Unless it's my name, of course."

"You can count me out," said Pam. "I don't want to have anything to do with it. Why should *you* decide? And why should you all listen to her?" she asked the others.

Eliza wondered why too, as she hurried over to piano practice. She knew Helen hoped it would be Eliza's name that was chosen.

But the name Helen drew from the four strips of paper she'd dropped into her beret was Carrie's. Eliza was first relieved for herself, then anxious for her friend, until she saw that Carrie didn't mind. She twirled around the dorm in her long pink dressing-gown, her braid flying out behind, pretending to be a ballet dancer. "Okay," she puffed, landing on Helen's bed, "what do I have to do?"

Helen paced the room. "Let's see, Turps. I dare you to . . . uhhh . . ." Eliza wondered if she was hesitating because she'd had a special dare just for Eliza in mind. ". . . to climb up to the Nursery by the roof."

"She'll fall!" said Pam at once. "That's too dangerous."

"No, she won't. It's dry tonight. I climbed down once, and up must be easier."

"Why not by the fire escape?" Eliza suggested. It was the first time she had spoken to Helen in over a week.

"It doesn't take much courage for *that*," replied Helen scornfully, looking away. Eliza reddened.

They all peered up at the slanted roof that led to the Junior Dorm above them.

"I can do that," said Carrie. "Should I come back the same way?"

Helen shook her head. "No, you'd better sneak down the stairs and stop off in the Red and Turquoise Dorms for safety. I know — send us a message on the Slipper Express when you get to the Turquoise Dorm and we'll let you know when the coast's clear."

The Slipper Express had been invented by Helen and Linda O., one of the grade sevens in the Turquoise Dorm. She was always called Linda O. to distinguish her from Linda I., although there wasn't much need for this. Linda I. was quiet and dull, while Linda O. was almost as boisterous as Helen herself.

The Yellow Dorm associated mainly with the two dorms of grade sevens and eights near them, with occasional forays into the Nursery above. No one on their side of the house had much to do with the three dorms of grade nines beyond Miss Tavistock's bedroom. They were too loathsome, pimply and fat and full of self-pity because of it.

Visiting between dorms was allowed only before dinner and on Sundays, so the Slipper Express enabled messages to be passed between the Yellow and Turquoise Dorms at other times. The slick hall floor was a perfect surface for a flat-bottomed slipper to coast along.

Now Helen wrote out a warning. "Carrie paying you a late-night call," she muttered. "Be prepared." She stuck the note inside one of Eliza's moccasins, the fastest slippers in the dorm, being both heavy and streamlined. Positioning it in the doorway, she sent the moccasin off with a strong push. It zipped down the hall and landed with a hollow thud at the other end.

Carrie hopped eagerly in her own fluffy slippers. "Shall I start now?"

"Go in bare feet, so you don't slip," said Eliza quickly. She shivered; the roof was steep and there was concrete below it.

Carrie sat on the wide windowsill facing them, only her legs inside and her hands gripping the bottom of the half-open window. She tipped her head back. "I just have to get a hold on the gutter," she called. Pulling herself up so they could see only her bottom half, she lifted one leg at a time onto the roof.

Eliza's heart beat in her ears as she leaned far out the adjacent window and watched Carrie scramble up until she disappeared. A squeal of alarm made her freeze; then she heard the sound of surprised laughter that meant Carrie had made it.

They went back to bed and waited for her return. Eliza knew *she* wouldn't have done it. Climbing trees was one thing, but this was much scarier. She wondered how her friend could be so brave. But Carrie never reflected about things; she just acted.

She was gone a long time, and Eliza started daydreaming about the ballet. It had been a revelation to her, even though they'd sat so high up the dancers had resembled a company of tiny dolls. There was something about their precise movements and the way their bodies and feet told a story that was deeply satisfying.

She tried to think of other things to take her mind off the dare. This morning they'd had Mark Reading. It seemed cruel, making everyone stand up in order as their marks were read out. But at least she had got mostly A's and B+'s — with one B in French — and she was secretly triumphant that she'd beaten Pam slightly. Later in the morning Miss Clark had praised Eliza's English exam. But then she'd read aloud with amusement her answer to a question about Tennyson's poem, "The Eagle": "The main impression in this poem is the sense of great height as the duck stands on a high rock and waits to strike."

A duck! Wherever had the word come from? She hadn't been thinking about ducks at all. She blushed violently, but the class's laughter was appreciative, not mocking. Eliza decided that strange things happen when writing under pressure.

Carrie and Jean had received respectable B's, but Helen had been among the group who remained sitting, their marks undisclosed, but below a C+. It was puzzling, how Helen rarely got her homework finished. The boarders had so much supervised prep that it was hard *not* to do it. In fact, Eliza had found that if she finished hers quickly she had time to sneak a book on top and read undisturbed.

Helen certainly seemed smart. Pam had been rehearsing for the inter-house spelling bee one night, and Helen had known all the words. "Why don't you enter it?" Carrie had asked her, but Helen had just replied it was too much trouble.

But Eliza didn't want to think about Helen.

Jean yawned. "Where *is* Carrie?" It was very late; Pam's eyes were closed, and Eliza would have liked to go to sleep herself.

WHAP! The slipper landed against the wall and startled them awake again. It wasn't Eliza's slipper, but a scruffy blue one. That was one problem with the Slipper Express: people forgot to send back the same one and you often had to retrieve your own the next day.

"Arrived okay. Safe to return?" read the message Helen pulled out. She stepped into the hall, listened for a second, then sent back an all-clear.

Suddenly they heard voices in the hall and froze. A few minutes later Carrie strolled through the door, calling over her shoulder, "Thank you, Miss Monaghan."

"What happened?"

"Did you get caught?"

"Shhh!" said Carrie. "Wait till she thinks I'm in bed." They waited five minutes.

"Now tell us," whispered Eliza urgently.

"Okay. It was really scary. I slipped once on the roof — did you hear me yell? My bathrobe got caught under my foot." Eliza winced.

"Then I rolled through the window onto Sandra's bed. Was she ever surprised! They thought it was wonderful and they wouldn't let me leave for a long time. I had to look at all their animals. I just love the juniors, especially Holly. They're so cute."

"Brats, not cute," growled Helen. "I know — I was with some of them last year. Go on!"

"I made it to the Red Dorm and talked to them for a while. Then I ran to the Turquoise Dorm and sent the message. But just as I was leaving I bumped into Matilda! She was coming up the stairs."

"Oooh, Carrie!" cried Jean. "What did you do?"

"I said — I said —" Carrie was laughing so hard she could hardly continue. "I said I had a headache and I was looking for her! And she got all gushy and called me a poor lamb and gave me an aspirin in her room."

"Did you swallow it?"

"I had to! I don't think it'll hurt me."

"Hurray for Turps!" said Helen, and all at once Eliza felt jealous.

Pam pulled her sheet over her head. "You are all being so dumb. Carrie could have broken her neck. Shut up now — I want to go to sleep."

"Prim P.J.," whispered Helen.

Eliza heard her and sighed. She wasn't tired any more, and she tiptoed into the bathroom with a book. Pam always complained when Eliza pulled the curtains back to get more light. She had tried reading under the covers with a flashlight, but the Pouncer had confiscated it.

She couldn't concentrate on her book. Adjusting the bathmat under her on the cold floor, she leaned back against the tub and thought about the dare.

Pam was right; it *had* been dangerous. Was it brave to do something foolhardy? She didn't think so, but Helen seemed to. Eliza was only glad she hadn't had a chance to call Eliza a goody-goody again. But not having to perform this dare just meant Helen would think up another one for her.

Eliza decided she didn't like Helen. At first the other girl had interested her, but they were too different to be friends. Carrie was much safer. Helen doesn't like me anyhow, she thought. And I don't care.

VII

Two Birthdays

"Would you like to have all your dorm-mates out for your birthday next week?" Aunt Susan asked one Saturday in November.

Eliza considered it. Carrie came out with her almost every week, so she would be included of course. It would be nice to have Jean, if she didn't mind missing a Saturday at home. But Helen and Pam — did she want them to intrude into her peaceful Saturday life? Nothing ever happened on her weekly visits with Aunt Susan and Uncle Adrian. It was always the same, and a lot like being in her own home. She preferred it that way.

But she knew her aunt and uncle wanted to meet the other three; she and Carrie were always discussing them. Also, it was Helen's birthday four days after Eliza's. Even if she wanted to, she couldn't very well leave her out.

"I'll ask them," she said finally. "But they might not be able to come."

Surprisingly, they all could. Jean said she could skip seeing her parents for one week, and she seemed pleased to be included. Pam, who usually went out with her friend Deb, said in a syrupy voice that Helen mocked, that she'd love to meet Eliza's relatives. Eliza was the most puzzled by Helen's acceptance. She didn't understand why the other girl would want to come, but Helen said it would be good to have some freedom. She began to act friendlier, even though Eliza remained aloof.

They were ready at the front door, holding their coats, at ten forty-five on Saturday morning.

"Don't you all look nice!" said Miss Tavistock, coming out of her study. "Many happy returns of the day, Elizabeth." She threaded her way through the rest of the crowd of boarders waiting to be picked up.

Carrie giggled. "What does that mean? You guys use such funny expressions." Carrie often pointed out what she considered to be Canadian oddities: French on the cereal boxes; singing "The Queen" at Friday afternoon assemblies; celebrating Thanksgiving in October; and saying "grade seven" instead of "seventh grade" and "dressing-gown" instead of "bathrobe." Sometimes Carrie's comments were irritating; it was as if she were laughing at Canada.

This morning, however, nothing could bother Eliza. It was her birthday. Before breakfast she had opened a parcel from her parents — two new books, a blue turtle-neck sweater and a fountain pen, something she'd wanted for a long time. Best of all, her birthday card contained a plane ticket to Toronto in December. Her mother had also sent a cake, which Eliza now balanced carefully in its box.

She felt older, but not too old. Twelve was the best age, she decided — still a whole year away from the terrors of thirteen, but more powerful than eleven.

They were all wearing one another's clothes. Eliza had Carrie's blue corduroy jumper on over her new sweater. It was too short, so she wore red tights with it. Eliza's kilt drooped on Carrie, but Carrie liked kilts and didn't have one of her own. Pam, who coveted Carrie's American clothes, had borrowed one of her flowery print blouses to match her own skirt. Jean's skinny figure was engulfed in Pam's fuzzy orange sweater-dress. Even Helen, who didn't care about clothes, had begged a baggy sweater from Eliza because she had nothing clean of her own to wear.

Eliza had lent it to her reluctantly. If she had to live all year with Helen, however, she couldn't ignore her completely. Instead she was carefully cool, and numbed herself to Helen's forceful presence. It was a rest to be so neutral.

Aunt Susan arrived with her baby and drove them downtown. They had a large, satisfying lunch at the Bon Ton. Carrie held the colicky baby on her knee all through the meal and bounced away her whimpers. Helen devoured three chocolate éclairs. Then Aunt Susan dropped them off at a movie, with careful instructions on how to get to her house on the bus.

There was time after the film to explore Granville Street. Eliza's aunt had never let her and Carrie come downtown alone before, and it made them feel important to be part of the bustling Saturday crowd.

Each of them chose a different store to go into. They looked at budgies (Jean), shoes (Pam), Chinese imports (Eliza), records (Carrie) and chocolates (Helen). In the last place the other four pooled their pocket money and bought Eliza peanut clusters for her birthday.

"It's great not to have a matron breathing down your neck," said Helen to Eliza as they waited for the bus. Eliza wondered again why she was being so agreeable. In spite of her resolution to remain unaffected, Helen's comment made her feel sorry for the other girl, being confined inside the school walls week after week. Almost all the boarders visited with friends or relatives on Saturdays, but Helen seemed to have nobody to sign her out.

The bus wheezed over the Granville Bridge and continued along Fourth Avenue. Eliza watched attentively for their stop. "It's so nice out," she said when they got off at Blenheim Street. "Do you want to see our secret beach? We don't have to be back at Aunt Susan's until five."

She had discovered the beach the first day she'd been in Vancouver, and since then she had shared it with Carrie every week. It wasn't really a secret, but no one else ever came there. Now, as they continued down Waterloo Street, across Point Grey Road and through the tiny park to the cement stairs, she felt proud at being able to show it off.

The steps were wet and mucky and Pam complained that her shoes were getting dirty.

"We keep jeans and old shoes at the Chapmans'," Carrie explained in a superior tone. "I wish we'd changed, Eliza." She seemed to be boasting that Eliza was her special friend; Eliza was surprised and flattered that Carrie, who seemed so confident, would do that.

It was a messy beach, littered with rocks, long pieces of driftwood and lumber thrown up by the tide. There was hardly any room for bare sand.

"I've seen lots nicer beaches than this!" said Pam scornfully. "You should see Hawaii — miles and miles of white sand."

"But look at the cliff!" said Eliza, who had only explored tame lake beaches before this year. "It's just like a cave." The bank was hollowed out as if by a spoon into even layers of blue, green and rust-coloured rock. Water dripped continually from the overhang and bushes hung down like vines.

They sat gingerly on the cold rocks that dotted the grassy mound Eliza privately called the look-out.

Where are the Lions?" asked Jean. Every Sunday, as the bus took them downtown to church, they looked for the two peaks that resembled sleeping lions. Here on the beach, it was too low to see them. Eliza stared dreamily at the snow-frosted mountains across the water; it was so clear that their lower slopes seemed covered in green fur. As she turned her head she could see the darker mass of Stanley Park, then the toy-like buildings of the city. Huge liners were anchored in the bay, as far out as she could look. Uncle Adrian said they came from all over the world. It was a view she never got tired of.

Shaking herself out of her daze, she handed round the peanuts and joined the discussion about *Mary Poppins*. Carrie, Pam and Jean raved about it.

"But it wasn't right!" objected Eliza. "They left out all the good parts of the book and added dumb songs instead. And Mary Poppins is supposed to be stern and plain-looking." Like Miss Tavistock, she mused.

Helen yawned. "*I* thought it was boring. Why didn't we go to *Tom Jones* instead?"

"Because we're too young, of course," said Pam. "But it wasn't boring. It was beautiful, all those old-fashioned clothes."

Jean turned apologetically to Eliza. "I *liked* the songs."

Even though the five of them were constantly together, it seemed odd for them to be together by choice. Eliza noticed new things. Carrie and Pam were the prettiest. Carrie was what Miss Bixley called a "true blonde," and her eyes were transparently blue. Pam looked like one of the healthy schoolgirls in *The Girls' Own Annual*, her dark curls blowing against her bright cheeks. Helen's face was pasty compared to theirs, as pale and puffy as a mushroom. No one could call her attractive, but she certainly stood out: her electric hair, huge glasses and largeness all drew attention to her.

Eliza wondered if *she* were pretty; the question had never occurred to her before. She decided that, like Jean, she was probably quite ordinary-looking.

Helen climbed down and began poking in the sand with a stick. "I bet there's rats down here," she said cheerfully. "Matilda told us she saw a rat on Second Beach last week."

"Rats!" The others drew up their feet in horror, except for Jean. She said she'd once tried to tame one that had lived in their garbage can. Eliza marvelled that Jean, so afraid of people, could be friends with a rat.

"Let's go back to your aunt's," said Pam with a shiver. "I'm freezing."

After dinner they sprawled, bloated with cake and ice cream, around the Chapmans' living room. Carrie was helping Aunt Susan put the baby to bed. Eliza pretended to watch TV with Pam and Jean, but she was really listening to Uncle Adrian talk to Helen behind her. He was showing her his fishing rods.

"I used to go fishing with my father all the time," Helen said eagerly. "At Nulki Lake. We caught rainbow trout. Have you ever used a fly called a Doc Spratley?"

Eliza was astonished at the enthusiasm in her voice. Who would have thought that Helen, of all people, liked fishing? Eliza liked it herself. She had to, in her family, her father and uncle were such fanatics.

On the way back to school in the car Uncle Adrian said, "In the spring, Helen, you'll have to come out with Eliza again and go salmon fishing with us." A yearning look flickered on Helen's face, then disappeared as she resumed her usual arrogant smile. Eliza flushed. Her uncle thought she and Helen were friends.

On Wednesday evening they celebrated Helen's birthday. After prep all the grade seven boarders were allowed to sit alone in the dining room and demolish the slab of chocolate cake that had "Happy Birthday, Helen" written on it in green icing.

Helen presided at the head of the table, flourishing the cake knife. "Chocolate, chocolate, dee-*lish*-us chocolate," she chanted. "P.J., have a huge piece. Sheila and Joan, pass your plates. There you are, Eliza Doolittle. Eat up, everyone, and rot your teeth!" A piece of icing flew off the knife and landed on Linda O.'s cheek. Helen at once daubed her own cheeks with icing, and the two performed a whooping war-dance around the table.

"Helen's so wild tonight," Carrie whispered to Eliza. "I guess she's happy because it's her birthday."

Eliza watched the red-headed girl flop down in her chair and concentrate on her cake. As far as she knew Helen had received no presents, but she'd seen her give some money to Miss Bixley to buy the cake. Perhaps the money was all she had got. Helen never talked about her family. Eliza had heard every detail about Carrie's brothers and sisters and parents; she knew Jean was an only child, and that Pam's brother went to boarding school in Toronto. But all she knew about Helen was that she came from a small city in central B.C.

That morning, after pondering the matter for some time, she had wished Helen a Happy Birthday. Helen grinned so widely that Eliza began to think she was wrong about her after all. It was as if Helen cast some kind of spell over her and she couldn't dislike her, no matter how much she tried to. Even if they weren't friends, it was a relief not to have to be her enemy.

"Now we're *all* twelve," said Helen, smacking her lips after her last swallow.

"I'll be thirteen in February," boasted Linda O., "and you're still the baby, Helen." The two of them were always exchanging insults.

"Well, we're coming along behind you as fast as we can, Linoleum!" retorted Helen. "And one day we'll be seventeen, and out of here! Free-e-e-e!" She slid a plate with a second piece of cake on it down the table to Linda O.'s place.

So Helen didn't mind growing older. Eliza was surprised, since Helen shunned teenage things as much as she did herself. The week before, the five of them had peeked in at the grade nines at their tea dance in the dining room. Each of the older girls was paired off with one of the boys who'd been sent over from St Martin's, the boys' school a few miles from Ashdown. Helen had made as much fun of the gyrating couples as Pam and Carrie had envied them.

Jean watched them wide-eyed, as if they were another species. Eliza had just gaped in dread. At home her friends were probably all going to dances. At least here the ordeal was delayed until you were fifteen.

Eliza licked the last cake crumbs off her plate. Carrie poked her and pointed to the window. "There's Madeline."

"I wonder why she's out of senior prep so early?" said Eliza. "I think I'll just go and say hello."

Slipping out of the dining room, and then the front door, she was just in time to meet her house captain at the top of the veranda steps.

"Hi, Eliza," smiled Madeline. "Can you help me carry these boxes over to the New Residence?"

"Do you think I'm allowed to?"

"Oh, I'm sure you are. Look, there's Bix . . . Miss Bixley, Eliza's just going to help me carry these — she'll be back soon."

Her arms full, Eliza trotted to keep up with Madeline's quick steps. "What's in the boxes?"

"All the costumes from last year's house plays. I thought I'd sort them out and see what we can use this year."

After they deposited the boxes in the hall Madeline invited Eliza into the Senior Sitting Room. Leading off it was a small kitchen.

"You seem to be having a lot of birthdays in your dorm," said Madeline, handing Eliza a cup of cocoa.

Eliza told her about her Saturday party and her presents, but inside she was feeling awed to be sitting here. The walls were plastered with posters of rock and roll stars. A sign on the refrigerator said "Lost! One gold hoop earring. If found, please return to Sharon before the Saints' dance on Saturday." Someone's red high-heeled shoe had been abandoned on the couch.

The room seemed soaked in the rumours that floated over to the Old Residence: that someone had pierced her dorm-mate's ears with a hot needle; that two girls had been caught smoking in the bathroom; that the grade elevens had mailed parts of a dissected frog they'd smuggled out of biology to Crewe, the boys' school on the Island.

"I don't want to grow up," Eliza blurted out suddenly.

"You're certainly doing a good job of it," teased Madeline. "Your uniform is already too short!"

"That's not what I mean."

Madeline's eyes lost their amused look. "Sorry," she said quietly. "I know — you don't want to be a teenager. I didn't either when I was twelve."

It was as if Madeline had read her mind. Eliza waved her hand around the room. "I don't! I hate all this stuff! Have you read the Narnia books?"

Madeline nodded.

"Remember when Susan doesn't go back to Narnia because all she's interested in is lipstick and nylons and invitations? I think it's right that she misses everything. She doesn't deserve to go back!"

"But Eliza, *that's* not growing up. It's not just being silly about boys and make-up and things."

Eliza wondered if Madeline had a boyfriend at home, as many of the seniors did. If she did, she never talked about it.

"You aren't like that," she said hopefully.

"Well, all I care about right now is becoming a pianist. It helps to know what you want to be — it gives you a reason not to go along with the crowd."

"I don't know," said Eliza. "I never think about it."

"Don't worry, you'll find out one day. Just enjoy being twelve."

"I do! But sometimes I think I shouldn't. Everyone else in grade seven is different from me. Even Carrie likes teenage things sometimes. Jean doesn't, but I bet Pam will change her." Eliza wondered why she was telling all this to Madeline and stopped, her face hot.

Madeline looked reflective. "Let's see . . . when I was your age I felt different too, but I guess I didn't care about it as much. It certainly must be *easier* to be like everyone else. Like wearing a disguise that you can throw off later when you don't need it. You and I just don't happen to like that disguise, all the things other people think is growing up. But that's all on the outside. I think real growing up's on the inside." She flushed. "But listen to me, I sound as if I know all about it. I'm only sixteen, you know."

Eliza, thrilled by the words "you and I," gazed at Madeline with uncritical admiration and pondered her words. She thought she understood the inside kind of growing up. It was like getting your period — something that was going to happen anyhow. The other kind, the outward disguise, was much more of a problem. She wished she had the confidence Madeline had to cope with it.

Madeline was looking embarrassed. "Listen, Eliza, I don't know what else to tell you. Being a teenager isn't always that great, but everyone has to go through it. Just don't worry about it! And one good thing about Ashdown is that it's easier to be yourself here. Don't you think so?"

Eliza wondered. The only people who accepted her as she was were the older ones — Madeline, Miss Tavistock and the teachers and matrons. Helen didn't. Carrie did so far, but she sometimes had conflicting interests. Just the other day she had been puzzled when Eliza didn't admire the new straight skirt her mother had sent.

But Madeline was partly right: the fact that there weren't any boys at Ashdown meant it was easier to change at your own rate. Eliza missed having boys in her classes. But it sometimes seemed, the older she got, that she wasn't allowed to be just friends with them anymore.

Madeline looked a bit desperate in the face of Eliza's solemn silence. "Eliza, you probably only feel different because you're younger than the others. But what about Helen? She just turned twelve too. Does she feel the same way?"

"She said she wanted to be seventeen!"

Madeline laughed. "I can't imagine Helen at seventeen. It's hard to predict what she'll turn out like. Are you two friends?"

"No . . . I'd like to be sometimes, but I don't think she does."

"How do you know unless you suggest it? I think you'd be good for Helen — she seems like a lonely kid."

This was something new to think about, along with everything else they'd discussed. Talking seriously with Madeline was like being with an older sister. Eliza ran back fast through the chilly darkness to the Old Residence, holding her cape open and pretending she was flying.

VIII

"See Amid the Winter's Snow"

Madeline's suggestion appealed to Eliza, but she didn't know what to do about it. She wasn't like Carrie. She couldn't just go up to someone and say, "Let's be friends." The rest of the term went by and Eliza and Helen remained on polite, but distant, terms.

Waking up before the bell one morning, Eliza wondered lazily if she should get up and be the first in the bathroom. But it was so toasty warm just lying curled up in bed. And something was different. The room felt muffled, as if it were lined in cotton batting. It was a familiar feeling that filled her with nostalgia, but what was it? Christmas coming? All at once she knew. In one movement she snatched open the curtains and bounded out of bed.

"Snow!" she yelled. There was a chorus of groans. "It snowed last night! Wake up, everyone, it snowed!" The lawn was a blanket of ghostly whiteness that shimmered in the dark. Eliza tore off her pyjamas and looked for her clothes. "Get up, Carrie. Come on, we've got to go out!"

"It's still night," murmured Pam. "Go back to bed."

"It's six-thirty," said Eliza. "Only half an hour before the bell. Come on, we can have a snowball fight! I didn't think it ever snowed in Vancouver!" Carrie and Jean got up sleepily, stumbled to the windows and admired the changed landscape. Pam opened her eyes and yawned. Helen, however, remained hidden under her tent of blankets.

"It never lasts," she mumbled from inside it. "Let me sleep. You'd think you'd never seen snow before, Eliza."

Eliza was ransacking her drawers. "I didn't think I would this year! If it's going to melt, let's go out now!" She paused and examined the grey lump that was Helen, then unrolled her recklessly from her cocoon, ignoring her protests. "Come on, quick, everyone get dressed! Hurry up, Pam!"

Pam surveyed her with astonishment. "Well! *You're* getting awfully bossy." But Eliza's excitement was contagious. In a few minutes they'd all struggled into an assortment of sweaters and jeans.

Carrying their boots, they crept past Miss Bixley's door, but Jean dropped one of hers and a small head stuck all over with curlers peered out. "What are you doing, girls? The rising bell hasn't even gone!"

"Oh, *please*, Miss Bixley, it snowed last night! Can't we go out and play in it until breakfast?"

"You'll get sopping . . . but I suppose it's all right. Be very quiet until you hear the bell, though."

Eliza was the first one out. She treaded the slippery veranda steps cautiously, paused at the top of the lawn, then propelled herself into the whiteness. The others ran after her and they dashed about silently, smothering their laughter with gloved hands and flinging the snow into the air.

It wasn't powdery like Edmonton snow, but clung to their jeans like glue. The trees looked as if they had been sprayed with soapsuds, and already the snow was slithering off them.

Everyone lay down and made snow angels. Eliza gazed up at the pewter-coloured sky and the silent old house full of sleeping girls, and suddenly she felt overwhelmingly, joyously alive. But the feeling passed and in a few seconds she was only conscious of how soaked her back was getting. She scrambled to her feet.

Inside the residences the bells commanded everyone to get up. It was exhilarating to be disobeying their orders for once. Eliza ran around in circles, her arms spread wide. A coil of tightness inside her — the pressure of these months with the new life she had chosen — sprung loose. She'd never known the tension was there until it was released. "Get u-u-u-u-up!" she shouted to the windows. "Get up, everyone, it snowed!"

"You're crazy!" grouched Helen, wiping moisture from her glasses with the end of her scarf. Helen hated getting up. "You're nuts, Eliza Doolittle. It's just a little snow." But she looked almost envious, and there was something vulnerable about her without her glasses on.

Eliza stuffed a handful of snow down Helen's back, and tossed more over her in a snow shower. "*You're* crazy!"

Helen cackled and went at Eliza with a snowball. They chased each other all over the lawn.

Windows opened around them.

"Look at the snow!"

"Look at the snow bunnies!"

"Come out, come out!" invited the Yellow Dorm. In a few minutes they were joined by more tousled boarders — all the juniors, most of the grade sevens and eights and quite a few seniors. Madeline was among them and Eliza pelted a snowball at her too. The snow was perfect for packing, the way it was only in the spring on the prairies.

A disorganized fight began, with volleys of icy missiles in all directions. Eliza was saturated. Her gloves and jeans stuck like a clammy second skin to her fingers and legs.

"Girls, girls!" On the balcony of the Blue Sitting Room stood Miss Tavistock, holding her coat around her like a shawl and trying to make herself heard above the screams of battle.

Even a snowball fight stopped for Miss Tavistock. Arms halted in the act of throwing and voices were stifled in mid-scream.

"I'm glad to see that someone is enjoying this dreadful snow, but you *must* be quieter. The neighbours will wonder what we're up to. Now you can play for ten more minutes, then I will ring the bell again and you must come in and get dry."

"Yes, Miss Tavistock," they chorused, and the skirmish continued in a more subdued manner.

The juniors were making a snow lady, dressing her in an Ashdown beret and scarf. Eliza joined them, her wild fervour disappearing. She was suddenly embarrassed by her own exuberance. It somehow didn't fit in with the ordered life she had become used to in the past three months.

By the end of the next day the snow had almost vanished, leaving only a few dirty patches on the edge of the driveway. But its coming made the last ten days of the term special. It was already an unusual time: Christmas exams were over and a holiday atmosphere prevailed. There was nothing to do but rehearse for the carol service.

As Eliza thought about flying to Toronto to join her family, she began to miss them more. Choosing presents in Woolworth's one Saturday she almost wept, she wanted to see them so badly. But it was a bearable kind of homesickness, a yearning that she knew would very soon be satisfied.

She liked the songs they were learning for the carol service even better than the daily hymns. There were old favourites, like "O Come All Ye Faithful," which sounded new and mysterious because they sang it in Latin. There were ones she'd never heard before, with curious words like "mickle" and "sweeting." The phrases in some of the carols were so perfect they made her spine tingle: "Earth stood hard as iron/Water like a stone."

Mr Whitney, the music teacher, was passionately concerned that they enunciate clearly. "Christ*mass*, girls, not Christ*muss!*" he entreated, his long hair flopping over his eyes. "And *let/us* — it's not a vegetable."

In Miss Clark's English class they spent a lot of time listening to her read aloud, having spelling bees, making Christmas cards and just talking about their plans for the holidays. After the well-regulated days crammed with lessons, this relaxed atmosphere was a novelty. Eliza had more time to talk to the day-girls and decided some of them weren't as snobby as she'd thought.

Even Miss Tavistock's class was slacker. The headmistress taught the seniors English, but the grade sevens got her only once a week, for scripture. It was the only time 7A and 7B met together. The larger-than-usual class was always on its best behaviour. Miss Tavistock had a way of quelling noise instantly: she just looked.

This week they didn't have to memorize another tedious Bible passage. Instead they discussed what Christmas meant.

"It's a time for loving everyone," said Pam virtuously. Usually they had to stand up to answer, but today they were allowed to speak without permission from their seats.

"You can't love *everyone*," mumbled Helen, who never opened her mouth in scripture if she could help it, since she hadn't usually done her homework.

"That's a very interesting comment, Helen," encouraged Miss Tavistock. "Do you mean you can't, or you shouldn't? I don't mean you personally," she added, "just people in general."

But Helen slouched in her seat and refused to continue. Someone else said you couldn't love Hitler, and a lively argument followed. This was the kind of discussion Eliza liked. She listened intently, although she was too shy to contribute. Then Miss Tavistock said that Christ loved Hitler, and Eliza squirmed. Scripture was interesting except when God entered into it. That seemed much too private a thing to discuss in a classroom.

While some grades were rehearsing their special carols, others were let loose for long gym periods or recesses. During one of these breaks, Eliza was walking around the driveway enjoying her box of raisins — a treat instead of their usual morning apple. She hummed the tune of "See Amid the Winter's Snow" to herself. The snow, however, had melted completely, and the weather was unusually mild. There was even a rose blooming at the back of the gym. It was hard to believe Christmas was only eleven days away.

"What are you doing, Eliza Doolittle?" Helen was sitting on the wall, her legs dangling over the outside. This was forbidden, but all the teachers were too busy to notice them. Eliza hoisted herself up beside her. The ivy prickled the backs of her bare knees.

"Are you — are you glad you're going home?" she asked hesitantly. They talked of nothing else in

the Yellow Dorm these days. Pam boasted about skiing in Switzerland. Jean was visiting her grandparents
in Kelowna and Carrie was going to Disneyland. But
Helen never took part in the excited chatter. Eliza
knew her question was nosy, but ever since the snowy
morning she'd felt easier with Helen, and she decided
to risk it.

Helen kicked the wall with her heel and dislodged
some ivy. "Glad? I hate it there!"

"Oh — but you're always saying you hate it
here!"

"I do. But home's worse."

Already Eliza wished she'd kept quiet. But after
a minute Helen continued, looking away. "They just
wanted to get rid of me, that's all."

"Who?"

"My mother and *him* — her new husband. My father died when I was seven, and then she married him
and I was in her way. So they shipped me off to boarding school. They said I was a problem, just because I
was caught stealing with a bunch of other kids. I didn't
even know they were stealing — I was just tagging
along. But my grandmother in Montreal said she'd pay
for Ashdown. She said it would be good for me. And
now I have a bratty half-sister, and as far as my mother
and step-father are concerned I don't even exist."

Helen had been talking faster and faster, spitting
out the words. She stopped abruptly and continued to
stare across the street.

Eliza was horrified. She had never known anyone
whose parents didn't like her. She remembered what

the day-girl in her class had said about being "a problem at home." That's what Helen was seen as — a problem, like a parcel, to be disposed of.

She had never known anyone as miserable as Helen seemed now, and she wanted to comfort her. It was the right time to declare her friendship, but for a moment she wondered what being friends with Helen would involve.

They sat there in silence, watching the cars drive by. Behind them a crow squawked, and faint singing drifted from the gym.

Finally Eliza put her hand on Helen's shoulder. She felt foolish, like someone in a story. Helen shrugged it off immediately, but she turned her head towards Eliza and blinked.

"You know, Eliza Doolittle, we should be able to really have some fun next term. We haven't played the Daring Game for ages! And you and I haven't even done one yet. And I don't think you're *really* a goody-goody," she added in a rush.

They were interrupted by an amused voice below them. "Now, what would Miss Tavistock say if she could see you!" It was somebody's mother, probably on her way in to collect a junior for lunch. Eliza and Helen exchanged a look of dignity and disdain. Smiling at the woman politely, they jumped off the wall.

On Friday afternoon at three o'clock Eliza waited, trembling, at the back of the cathedral. She wiped her palms on her Sunday skirt and listened to the opening

notes of the first carol. Two navy-blue lines of Ashdown students, beginning with the tiny grade ones and
ending with the head girl, resplendent in her red blazer,
began the slow processional down the aisle.

"Once in royal David's city" was like "Once upon
a time," the beginning of the story they would tell in
readings and carols. Eliza stepped lightly in time. In the
first verse, which they sang without accompaniment,
their voices sounded thin and frail in the huge space.
Then the organ joined in and they added harmony,
getting louder as the story progressed. Eliza spotted
her aunt and uncle in the congregation, grinned at
them and sat down in her place as one of the seniors
began the first reading.

The church was a tranquil retreat from the buzz of
traffic outside. Every Sunday for fourteen weeks Eliza
had daydreamed in one of its front pews, not paying
much attention to the service but savouring the pre-
cious hour of privacy. She knew every detail of the
church, its dark interlacing beams, the stone arch of
the chancel, the black-and-gold lanterns and the richly
coloured stained glass windows. The eagle was her favourite: he held the Bible on his back while he peered
sideways, his claws splayed on a golden ball. As she
watched him she would anticipate hungrily Sunday
dinner's deep apple pie with its gooey crust.

Today it felt good to be active, to give something
back to the cathedral after months of soaking up its
peace. She rose and sat as the service continued, singing out clearly into the depths of the building.

Madeline was one of the shepherds, and Eliza watched her proudly when she and the others stood to speak. "Let us now go even unto Bethlehem, and see this thing which is come to pass," they intoned. It was perfect; they didn't even say "lettuce."

Madeline looked very small, standing between the other two girls. Eliza felt a surge of affection for her. If she hadn't come to Ashdown she never would have known Madeline — or Carrie, or Helen. She was excited about going home to her family, but it was also good to have friends to come back to. There had been a few difficult times in the first term, but they had all been centred on Helen. Now that she and Helen were going to be friends, the rest of her time here would be fine. She was glad she'd be able to tell her parents that coming to Ashdown had been the right decision.

"Ha-a-a-ail thou ever blesséd morn!" Eliza sang as they stood up again. The service was almost over, which meant it was almost time for the holidays to begin. Miss Tavistock, in a green suit, gazed at them intently from the front row, looking as if she were waiting for something to go wrong. Eliza hoped she was pleased.

Everyone was excited now and exchanged eager glances as the organ played the prelude to the last carol. "Hark the herald angels sing!" Eliza shouted as they marched back down the aisle. She was filled with the magic feeling that came every year. Finding Aunt Susan and Uncle Adrian in the church hall, she hugged them a breathless goodbye.

Then she was whisked into the bus by Miss Bixley and hurried through the dark wet streets back to school. Then out again in a taxi to the airport, and to the plane that would carry her across the country to her family.

Part II

Winter

IX

A Poor Beginning

"Eliza, Eliza, you're back!" Carrie almost knocked Eliza over as she rushed at her. Eliza put down her suitcase and attempted a smile. She nodded to Jean, unpacking in a corner. But only a tiny part of her was pleased to see them again. The familiar yellow room was not as welcome a sight as she had expected, and she didn't understand why.

For a moment she was distracted by Jean's hair. A brown frizzy halo that looked like a matted bird's nest circled her thin face. "What happened to you?" blurted out Eliza before she had time to be more tactful.

"My mother permed it," said Jean sadly. "She thought it needed more body."

"Don't worry," said Carrie. "Just wash it a lot, and when it grows you can cut all the curl off. It doesn't look that bad. I'll lend you a ribbon to flatten down the top."

Jean looked grateful, although they all knew there was nothing much she could do about it. Eliza had met Jean's mother several times on Saturday mornings. She was a brisk, scary woman. It would be hard to resist her if she decided to do something to your hair.

That made her think of her own mother, who had driven her to the airport after they'd dropped off the twins at her grandparents' and her father at work. Before Eliza had boarded the plane she had held her mother close, snuggling into her soft fur jacket and trying not to cry.

She felt like crying now, not joining into the hilarity as Pam stepped into the dorm bearing a gigantic pink rabbit. What's wrong with me? Eliza thought irritably. Why aren't I glad to be back?

Helen arrived last, dumping her bags on the floor with a clatter. "Scotty, what on earth have you done to your hair? We'll have to iron it for you. P.J., get that disgusting rabbit off my bed. Hi, Eliza Doolittle — glad to be back in this dump?"

Eliza shrugged. But Helen's banter cheered her up slightly, and she couldn't help grinning at the other girl's extraordinary appearance. Under her skimpy coat Helen was wearing a purple turtle-neck T-shirt and an unpressed red tartan skirt. Over these hung an orange garment that looked like the top of a set of long underwear. Woolly green tights, with her navy school socks pulled up over them, and brown rubber boots completed the outfit.

It was amazing that Helen's mother would allow her daughter to look so awful. Mothers again . . . Eliza tried to think of something else.

Miss Bixley, who had a bad cold, hurried them about between sniffs. Eliza found herself resenting the fussy orders. "Come along now — all suitcases to be unpacked by four-thirty, then a drawer inspection."

It's like an army, thought Eliza. Ashdown had never seemed like this before.

"Let's apple-pie Bix's bed!" suggested Helen when the matron had left them.

"Not when she's sick," objected Carrie. "That's mean."

"No it's not. She'll just laugh. She always does. Come on, Eliza, before she gets back."

Eliza agreed with Carrie. Miss Bixley probably just wanted to crawl into her bed early tonight, without having to re-make it. But she *felt* mean. And Helen was her friend now and she obviously expected Eliza to join her.

"Okay." Eliza laughed recklessly, ignoring Carrie's surprised look. Carrie didn't know yet that Eliza and Helen were friends; the conversation on the wall had happened too near the end of term.

Helen chortled as they tucked in Miss Bixley's top sheet deftly, folding up the bottom of it, and covered it again with the blankets. "You're good at this, Eliza Doolittle! Who taught you?"

"Oh, I don't know." Eliza surveyed the neatly-made bed glumly. It only made her feel worse.

As the day went on, she realized that the heaviness she felt was a swelling homesickness that filled her until she wanted to explode. But she held it tightly inside her until Lights Out, until the others had stopped listing their Christmas presents and the dorm was still. Outside the foghorn sounded its two mournful notes: *uuuuuuuuh oh*. Eliza couldn't hold back her tears any longer. They streamed down her cheeks and into her ears as she lay on her back and tried not to let the others hear.

Memories of the holidays marched relentlessly through her mind. It had been a perfect Christmas, crammed with treats: visits to grandparents and cousins, skiing at Collingwood, the *Nutcracker* at the O'Keefe Centre and explorations of downtown Toronto. Best of all was just sitting around the kitchen of the duplex the Chapmans had rented, fondling Jessie and chattering endlessly to her parents. She had soaked up her family as thirstily as a dry sponge. Even the Demons were tolerable, for they'd begun to talk. They were normal people now, two brothers with whom she could have a real conversation.

They had turned the den into a bedroom for Eliza. She would never forget the first night she had shut the door and recaptured the peace of being utterly alone. The burden of four other people's personalities continually rubbing against hers had dropped away instantly. What was surprising was how little she had missed privacy until she got it back.

Still, all through the two weeks she had thought about returning to Ashdown with happy anticipation and talked eagerly about the school to her parents. She knew they were comfortable now about her being there.

"You've grown up a lot," said her mother one day. "I think boarding school has made you more confident."

Everything had been fine until the moment of saying goodbye in the airport, when this overwhelming yearning had flooded her without warning. When the plane rose from the ground she wanted it to turn around and go back. The stewardess had treated her like a small child, telling her when to undo her seat-belt and bringing her special drinks. Eliza *felt* young and, for the whole of the five-hour flight, very alone. As she passed over the snow-bound country, she tried not to think of the family she was leaving behind her. In the fall this had been easy, for she hadn't been able to visualize them anywhere. Their apartment, and Toronto, had been hazy in her mind. But now she could imagine exactly what they would be doing at any moment.

The other four were sleeping quietly. Clasping her hands tightly over John, Eliza pressed him to her chest but wished he were Jessie, something warm and alive. John's button eyes, which she had often imagined full of life, glinted blankly in the dark, offering no help.

She wiped her eyes on John's ears. What should she do? Phone her parents and say she wanted to come back to Toronto? They would be sympathetic, but puzzled. She hated to worry them or to admit she was wrong. There was a horrible certainty inside her that, even if she did return, nothing would ever be the same. She could never be a little girl living at home again — she'd left home. It was too late to undo that. Why did they let me come? she thought angrily. I *am* too young for boarding school.

By Toronto time it was very late, but she couldn't sleep, and it was getting more and more difficult to stifle her sobs. She heard Miss Bixley going into her room . . . the bed!

Eliza got down and padded to the door, startling the matron. "Heavens, Eliza, you gave me a fright! Is something wrong? Here, come into my room so we don't wake the others."

"Oh, Miss B-Bixley . . ." As the door closed Eliza finally let her wild sobs loose. She tried to talk, but her lips were trembling too much.

"Goodness me, child! Come and sit down." Miss Bixley sat Eliza on the bed, wrapped her afghan around her, handed her a tissue and took one herself. They both blew their noses.

"We-we apple-pied your bed — and I'm so s-sorry — and I miss my parents — and I don't like being back here . . ." Eliza sobbed for a few more minutes while the matron made cocoa on her hot-plate.

"Dear me, Eliza, you've certainly taken a long time to get homesick, haven't you?" she said in her matter-of-fact way. "You'd think this was the first term, not the second!"

Eliza snuffled and gasped for air. "Everything was ex-exciting the first term. Now it just seems the same. And I didn't know how much I m-missed them until I saw them."

"You'll get over it. And you don't know what will happen this term — why it's barely begun! Now you wouldn't want your parents to worry about you, would you?" Miss Bixley handed her a steaming cup of cocoa. Eliza curled her cold fingers around it.

She felt disjointed. One part of her was still sobbing, but she was frightened of how much crying was left inside her and forced herself to stop. Another part, strangely detached from her shuddering body, was watching herself sniff and gazing at Miss Bixley's room. It was crowded with small luxuries: fat cushions, shirred pink lampshades and a sheepskin rug.

"I shouldn't tell you this, I suppose," said the matron, settling down in her wicker rocking chair, "but you're lucky you have a family you feel homesick *for*. I've never met your parents, Eliza, but from the way you talk about them they sound like very nice people. Some girls who come here haven't got such happy home lives."

"Like Helen," murmured Eliza. She felt numbed and embarrassed now and was glad to talk about someone other than herself.

"Yes, that poor child has been on her own since she was nine. And Pam isn't so fortunate either."

"Pam?" Eliza was surprised; Pam's parents seemed to give her anything she wanted.

"I've met her parents, and a snooty pair they are. I don't suppose Pam gets much real affection."

Eliza's curiosity was aroused, and she hoped the matron would go on. Miss Bixley was gossiping as if Eliza were her own age.

"Now Jean's parents are cold fish — that's the Scottish in them, I expect. My brother-in-law was the same way. They expect too much of Jean. They think this school is going to turn her into something she isn't. She'd be far better off living at home. But Jean's a solid person underneath. She'll survive."

Eliza had no idea that Miss Bixley thought about them all so much. Even through her dazed misery she couldn't help being fascinated. "What about Carrie?" she asked.

"Carrie's got very pleasant, warm parents — but you met them on Remembrance Day, didn't you? She's one that boarding school's probably good for, being the youngest of such a large family and a touch spoiled. And she seems to like it here."

"Is it — is it good for me, do you think?"

"Well, let's see . . ." Miss Bixley looked at Eliza appraisingly. "You're more sensitive, but you're sensible too. A tricky combination."

She stopped rocking and became Eliza's matron once more. "But goodness me, look at the time! Now Eliza, the best thing you can do is to be your usual cheerful self. There's nothing wrong with being homesick, but don't you feel better after a good cry?"

Not really, Eliza wanted to say; she hadn't been able to cry long enough to feel better. Because Miss Bixley expected her to, however, she nodded.

"Thank you, Miss Bixley," she mumbled. "Should I make your bed again?"

"You're bad girls, you and Helen . . . oh, I know

Helen must have helped you. No, I'll make it. You get off to bed."

The next morning the familiar Sunday routine grated on Eliza in a way it never had before. It seemed ridiculous to stand in the Blue Sitting Room and hold up your hands, palms out, for nail inspection. If the Pouncer could see your nails over the tops of your fingers she sent you back upstairs to cut them.

The bus going to the cathedral resounded with eager stories of the holidays, but Eliza barely heard Carrie's account of Disneyland. From the bridge she stared out at the gloomy grey sea. And in church she could not help thinking that, by Toronto time, her parents would have finished lunch and the Demons would be napping.

That afternoon Madeline came over to the Old Residence especially to see Eliza. She asked her to be in charge of collecting the house cards for Cedar this term and smiled as she inquired about Eliza's holidays, but she seemed distracted, as if she were thinking about something else. For the first time, Eliza felt unimportant to Madeline. She's not really interested in me, she thought.

Miss Tavistock stopped Eliza on the stairs after rest with a strong handshake and her usual cheerful greeting: "Welcome back, Elizabeth. How was your holiday? All ready to start a brand new term?" Eliza had meant to show the headmistress the stamp album she had received for Christmas. But now she was afraid to be too friendly, in case she cried again. There was no point in telling either Madeline or Miss Tavistock about her homesickness. There was nothing they could do about it.

Miss Tavistock was in a very different mood that evening. After supper she made all the Old Residence boarders assemble in the Blue Sitting Room. "I am sorry to have to begin the term with a lecture," she said stonily, "but something very upsetting has been brought to my attention. Mrs Renfrew has informed me that someone has been stealing money from the Pound Box. Since it is kept in your laundry room, it must have been a member of this residence who did it. This is a very serious matter, girls. I want everyone to sit here and think about it while I speak to you individually. If the person responsible has the courage and honesty to confess, I will not divulge her name."

Eliza had never seen the headmistress like this. Miss Tavistock's eyes were fiery, and her voice was deadly calm. There was truth, then, in the warnings she had heard about her last term.

They had to go one at a time into her study to be questioned. When it was her turn Eliza was irritated that the headmistress made her feel guilty when she had never stolen anything in her life. It was just one more thing to add to her increasing misery. Miss Tavistock was not so perfect after all.

"Are you certain you have not been near the money, Elizabeth?"

"*No*, Miss Tavistock!"

"I do have to ask everyone, Elizabeth, so I would appreciate it if you didn't answer as if you were insulted." The headmistress's voice was strained and her face was white. Eliza whispered an apology, wishing she could just go to bed and cry again.

But she had to return to sit with the rest of the silent boarders. Carrie rolled her eyes, but Eliza wouldn't respond and pretended not to notice her friend's hurt look. The ticking of the hall clock seemed to fill the whole room.

Finally Miss Tavistock confronted them again. "I am extremely disappointed. Since no one seems willing to confess now, I only hope that whoever took the money will come to me later. You will certainly not get the ice cream Mrs Renfrew was going to buy for you with it. This is a very poor beginning to the term, a poor beginning indeed." She marched out.

After Lights Out, Helen couldn't stop talking about it. "It's so unfair. How does she know it's one of us? It could be a senior, or a day-girl — even a matron! I bet the Pouncer took it herself so she wouldn't have to spend it on us."

But the others were too subdued by the incident to comment. When a message arrived on the Slipper Express — "What a drag! Charlie's a pain to take up all our TV time" — no one even bothered to answer.

X

Being Bad

Eliza wasn't used to being unhappy. She turned to her daily classroom activities with dull relief and tried to ignore the feeling of wretchedness inside her. Miss Bixley had said she'd get over it. She waited for the heaviness to lighten and wondered how long it would take. The first weeks of the year seemed to have a cloud over them, like the cloud that hovered endlessly over the city, pouring down rain.

"It's the worst term," complained Miss Bixley, wringing out Helen's socks after their walk. "So dark and wet and you all in bad moods from being cooped up so much. I'd rather have snow than this incessant downpour."

Eliza agreed fervently. At least you could go out and *play* in the snow. For ten days they'd had their breaks indoors, boxed up in the school basement like restless animals.

The only times she liked now were the Saturdays when the school took them skiing on Seymour Mountain. Skiing was the only sport she'd ever been good at; her father had first taken her to the Rockies when she was six. Zooming down the hill was like flying, and the wind rushing in her face blew away her homesickness for a while. But even high up on the mountain they were often rained out.

"We need a dare," said Helen one Sunday evening when the Yellow Dorm were cleaning their oxfords.

"I'm game," said Eliza at once. She had to do something to relieve the tedium of this term.

"I'm not," said Pam predictably. "Helen, you're not supposed to use that bottled stuff. It cracks when it's dry."

"It's much easier than all that rubbing," said Helen calmly. She continued to ooze black liquid out of a sponge-tipped bottle onto her shoes and the floor as well.

Carrie spat on the leather of her second shoe, then polished it glossy. "Do I have to put my name in again, since I've already done one?"

"No — just Eliza and Jean and me."

I hope it's my name, thought Eliza as Helen shook the beret containing the three slips of paper.

It was. A welcome eagerness stirred inside her; it seemed a long time since she had felt this kind of excitement.

Helen didn't consider very long. "Okay, Eliza Doolittle. I dare you...to lose a house point."

"Oh no!" gasped Jean who, like Eliza, had never lost a house point. "That's too much."

Carrie agreed. "I don't think the dares should be things to do with the school. Just the dorm."

"She wouldn't do it, anyway," said Pam. "Would you, Eliza?"

"How about it, Eliza?" Helen grinned at her confidently. "I've lost six so far this year. It's not that drastic."

"I've *never* lost a house point," stated Pam firmly. "And I never will. If you want to let down your house for a silly game, Eliza, all I can say is I'm glad you're not in Hemlock."

"Don't do it, Eliza," pleaded Carrie. "When I lost one for talking in the hall it was terrible, confessing it in front of everyone."

Eliza listened to them silently, observing the circle of their waiting faces. A strange recklessness surged up in her. Why *not* try to lose a house point? She was tired of being good all the time. The biggest problem was disappointing Madeline, but she put that out of her mind. And besides, Madeline was distant this term. She went around with a dreamy look on her face and barely seemed to notice Eliza.

Tossing her head, Eliza said, "All right. I'll do it. How long do I have?"

"A week," said Helen gleefully. "*I* could lose one in half an hour, but you'll have to try harder — they aren't used to watching you."

Helen was right. Eliza began on Monday morning with the most common offence: talking in prayers. She

whispered to her neighbour, who refused to answer.
The prefect standing beside 7A, looking distinguished
in her special light blue blazer, seemed lost in a day-
dream and didn't even notice. Eliza spoke again in the
line back to the classroom, to the same girl, who hissed
"Shhh!" in annoyance. But the tall prefect who was
stationed outside only called out, "No talking, please."
What was the matter with them? Usually they were
eager to pounce on the grade sevens, whom they said
needed to be whipped into shape after being coddled
in the Junior School.

For the rest of the day she continued to talk in the
wrong places — in the hall, in class and in the cloak-
room. Either no one noticed, or they simply asked her
to be quiet, with a surprised look at the usually well-
behaved Eliza.

She sat alone at tea after classes were over for the
day, trying to think of all the crimes she could com-
mit. It had to be something in school; the house point
system didn't apply in the residence.

Not doing your homework — Helen had lost several for that. But it was one area of her life Eliza knew
she couldn't fudge. Being good at her schoolwork was
her only security these dreary days; she didn't want to
lose the soothing self-respect it gave her.

Rudeness to teachers or prefects. That would be
difficult to pretend too; she wasn't a very good actor.

Forgetting your books. Being late. Being untidy.
Now those all had possibilities. She slurped her milky
tea thoughtfully.

"Read your tea leaves, Eliza?" Roberta, a plump
grade nine boarder, sat down beside her. All the

grade nines were reading tea leaves. It was their latest fad. Eliza didn't believe in it, but she turned the thick white cup over onto its saucer and rotated it the required three times.

"I see . . . I see . . ." murmured Roberta, gazing into the flecked pattern of the tea leaves meaningfully, ". . . that tomorrow you are going to do something unusual."

"You're right — I am! Thanks, Roberta." Eliza got up, leaving the girl staring into the teacup with surprise. Her predictions didn't usually get such an enthusiastic response.

Tuesday was uniform inspection day. After lunch all the students had to line up in their classrooms while prefects checked for brushed blazers, crisp blouses, sharp pleats and shiny shoes. Two or more areas of sloppiness almost guaranteed a lost house point. Eliza was going to make sure there would be no wavering over her.

It was easy to look messy, being difficult enough to look tidy at the best of times. Her oxfords were, unfortunately, already polished, but she scraped her toes along the pavement of the driveway on her way back from practising and shuffled through a pile of muddy leaves before she came in. For the rest she had to wait until fifteen minutes after breakfast when they were allowed back in the dorm to collect their things for school.

Hidden in the bathroom away from the others, whom she could hear brushing their blazers, Eliza wet her skirt and stretched out the pleats in the damp patches. She had saved a bit of toast, loaded with marmalade, from breakfast. Dribbling it down the front of her blouse, she covered it up with her sweater. Then she pulled her cape around her and hurried over to school.

Later in the day at the back of the classroom, after a lunch where she had managed to spill soup on her blazer without even trying, Eliza got ready for inspection. She took off her sweater, ripped open part of the hem of her skirt and threw away the elastic bands that held up her socks. Then she joined the line of waiting students.

Just her luck to get Sarah, the nicest and most understanding of all the twelve prefects. "That's an unusual way of wearing your sweater, Louise . . . Oh, I know you like a round-necked look better, but don't you think the V at the back will look funny when you take your blazer off? . . . Carol, your blouse is rather rumpled . . . Ah, Pam, neat as a pin as usual. Oh! Eliza!"

Everyone stared at Eliza as Sarah perused her in astonishment. Maybe I overdid it, she thought sheepishly, as she saw herself through their eyes: scuffed dusty shoes, socks slumped around her ankles, drooping puckered skirt, blouse smeared with a rusty stain and blazer splashed with congealing spots of green pea soup.

"Eliza, you're not the tidiest person around, but I've never seen you look like this! Are you having a bad day? Is something wrong?"

Sarah's kindness was exasperating. Just take off a house point and get it over with, thought Eliza. Since the prefect expected an answer she mumbled, "I don't know."

Sarah continued to gaze at her in wonder. "Hmmm . . . I don't know either. You know, Eliza, you should lose a house point for this — even two! But you usually at least *try* to be neat. I'll let you off this week, but next Tuesday you must be perfect — not a thing wrong — or I will take one off. Okay?"

Eliza didn't want to lose a house point *next* week. It would be too late for the dare then. Sarah sent her off to tidy up before the bell. She was so worn out from her experiment that she gave up trying to be bad for the rest of the day.

"Want some ideas? I'd be glad to give you some," offered Helen that night after Pam had told the others how Eliza had looked.

"No, I'll do it myself," said Eliza stubbornly. It amazed her that it was so difficult. Once you had acquired a reputation for good behaviour, people didn't see you any other way.

Forgetfulness and lateness were still possibilities. On Wednesday morning she forgot her French book, but Mme Courvoisier simply sent her all the way back to the dorm to get it. On Wednesday afternoon she deliberately left her clean gym clothes in her desk, but half the class had also forgotten theirs. Mrs Lomax was so exasperated she made them do circuit training, which they hated, instead of letting them try out the new trampoline.

It must happen today, thought Eliza on Thursday. Tomorrow was house meeting day; if she didn't lose a point until then she'd have to wait a whole week until she apologized publicly for it, and she couldn't bear that. It should be easy enough to be late for something — and that was her last resort.

After the afternoon break, once more an indoor one spent in the stuffy cloakroom that smelled of wet wood, Eliza slipped into the downstairs bathroom and sat on a toilet seat for ten minutes by her watch. Then she walked down the hushed corridors with a beating heart.

Behind each closed door droned a teacher's voice. She could hear Miss Tavistock reciting a poem to the grade elevens in ringing tones: "I am the master of my fate/I am the captain of my soul." Eliza tried to make her wobbly knees move faster without her shoes resounding any louder on the parquet floor.

Standing outside her classroom door, she listened to them read their parts from *A Midsummer Night's Dream*. Eliza was Bottom, and she wished desperately that she were already in there, waiting to speak. But it was too late now. She opened the door.

"Elizabeth, where on earth have you been?" The voices stopped and Miss Clark, usually kind, looked up crossly.

Eliza had forgotten to think of a reason. This was all getting much too complicated; she wished she'd never accepted Helen's dare. "I'm sorry, Miss Clark," she stammered. "I-I was reading a book in the cloak-room and I forgot the time."

"You shouldn't be so absent-minded. You can bring me your house card after class. Sit down now and get ready to read."

So it was done. Eliza's face burned as she bent over her Shakespeare. She was relieved that the first part of the dare was accomplished, but facing the consequences would be even worse.

First she had to take up her green house card, already fuller than most in the plus column, to Miss Clark to fill in. "Unpunctuality," the teacher wrote swiftly. She looked as if she were about to say some-thing, but then she initialled and dated the card and handed it back without a word.

"You did it! Welcome to the club," whispered Helen at dinner. They were at the same table that month, and tonight, surrounded by three seniors debating loudly the number of calories in junket, they could talk with-out being overheard.

Eliza played with the slippery white blobs of her dessert. Usually she enjoyed it, but tonight she wasn't hungry. "I wish I hadn't. Tomorrow's going to be awful — I feel like a phoney."

"You're still much too good — but I'll change you. Can I have your dessert if you're not going to eat it?"

On Friday morning Eliza crept by the large house point chart outside Miss Tavistock's office in the school. She

glanced quickly at the "1" that had been written
beside her name. At least it was the end of the week
and it would only be up for a day. It was embarrassing, but also oddly thrilling, to see it there.

House meetings began at one o'clock. The list of
persons who had lost house points was read first, right
after the Minutes.

Eliza decided to be a knight, confessing a necessary disloyalty to the rest of the Round Table. Standing in front of the room full of curious faces, she
pulled back her shoulders and held her head high.
What was it she'd heard Miss Tavistock say? "I am
the captain of my fate" — something like that. She
avoided catching Madeline's eye. The house captain
was standing behind the desk looking solemn, as she
always did on house meeting days.

There were five other offenders in line with her.
The recitation began. Eliza quickly counted and saw
that she would be third.

"I'm sorry I lost a house point — I was eating on
the street."

"I'm sorry I lost a house point — I lost my hymn
book."

Her turn now. "I'm-sorry-I-lost-a-house-point-I-
was-late-for-class."

She watched Madeline conduct the rest of the
meeting, but barely heard a word of it. At the end she
collected all the house cards — her new responsibility, which today seemed like a farce — and handed
them to Madeline with a trembling hand.

"Can you stay a moment?" Madeline smiled encouragingly. Eliza shut the door and sat down on top of one of the front row desks.

"I'm sorry, Madeline!" she exclaimed, no longer a misunderstood young knight but ashamed and guilty. "It was all a mistake."

"But don't worry about it, Eliza! That's what I wanted especially to tell you. Everyone's late for classes — everyone loses house points. You care too much. It's not that important. And it's not as if you did it on purpose."

Oh, but I did, I did! thought Eliza. It was so confusing. One house point wasn't important, and she'd certainly earned enough for Cedar to more than make up for it. But what she'd done seemed important in a way she didn't want to understand.

At least Madeline was paying attention to her again. And she wasn't upset. But even that baffled her: her house captain should surely care the most.

It was a relief to have it over, this tense week when she'd felt like another person. She didn't have to try to misbehave any longer, although she'd better remember to have her uniform in order next Tuesday. Still, even losing another house point wouldn't be so awful now.

It all suddenly seemed trivial. She could never take it so seriously again, even though she wished she could. Why was everything at Ashdown changing so much?

"You know," Madeline said, as she tallied the cards, "I sometimes think this whole house point system is petty. Like some English schoolgirls' story."

"I've read those books!"

"Do you think Ashdown's like that?"

"I used to — now I'm not sure." Eliza could feel herself wanting to pour out her disillusionment to Madeline, but she didn't want her house captain to think she was disloyal. Madeline would likely be a prefect next year. She *must* believe in the system. She was probably saying these things just to make Eliza feel better.

"Is anything wrong, Eliza?" asked Madeline as they left for classes. "You seem kind of blue these days."

Eliza shook her head.

Madeline bent over her books, her veil of hair hiding her face. "I'm sorry we haven't had any time to talk this term. I have a lot of things on my mind right now, but I'm always willing to listen. Are you sure there's nothing wrong?"

Whatever secret Madeline had made Eliza feel even more isolated. "Oh no," she said stiffly, forcing a smile. "Nothing's wrong at all."

Friday was Helen's bath night. While she was out of the dorm Pam said to Eliza, "I think Helen's a bad influence on you. Last term you never would have acted the way you did this week."

Carrie looked at Eliza reproachfully for a second and added quietly, "I think so too."

"She's not!" said Eliza, flushing. "I chose to do it, didn't I?"

It was none of their business. She didn't care

what Pam thought, but Carrie's comment stung. It occurred to her that she'd hardly spoken to Carrie all week, she'd been so busy conferring with Helen. Perhaps juggling her two friends was going to be a problem — one more, on top of all the others.

XI

Solitary Saturday

Eliza began to feel a leaden pride in the way she managed to shove her homesickness deep inside her. Saturdays were the most difficult days. Uncle Adrian looked so much like her father that she felt a pang every time she looked at him. And Aunt Susan was so fussy, it made her long for her easygoing mother all the more.

Every Sunday she had to struggle with herself before writing to her parents. She yearned so badly to pour out her misery to them that she forced herself, instead, to write long cheerful accounts about every detail of school life.

She discovered a trick to keep the awfulness from rising: Each time she felt it she made herself contemplate starting a new school somewhere in Toronto. This was so horrifying an alternative that it pushed the longing for her family away for a while. Gradually she became resigned to carrying the heaviness around inside her, like an unwelcome guest who wasn't going to leave. And, as the half-way point in the term approached, it didn't seem so interminably long until she could return to Toronto for Easter.

By contrast, Helen was becoming more high-spirited every day. Giddy with energy, she ran everywhere, knocking things over and earning exasperated scoldings from the matrons, which she shrugged off carelessly. Behind her glasses her eyes glittered with charged excitement. It was difficult to see what she could find so stimulating about these dull days, but her exuberance cheered up Eliza.

The last dare had cemented their friendship. The two of them spent much of their free time, when they could get out of games in the gym, in the cape cupboard by the front door: a perfect hiding place Helen had discovered two years ago. "No one else knows about this," she confided. "Not even Linoleum — she'd just tell everyone."

Huddled at the end of the narrow cupboard, they were totally concealed. Even if someone opened the door, it was too dark to notice them, and they'd strung an extra cape from one wall to the other to make sure. The space behind it was as snug as the inside of a tent. They sat on the dusty floor and pursued the endless topic of everyone else at school.

Helen did most of the talking, and Eliza was glad to be distracted from her depression by the other girl's stories. "We really fooled Fidget," she said with satisfaction one day. "She always sits on the edge of her desk with her feet dangling in the wastepaper basket. Nancy put an alarm clock in it and Fidget's foot set it off! She was furious! But she didn't know who'd done it, so she just yelled at us for a while and gave us extra homework."

Eliza shuddered. Mrs Fitch's tirades were famous and she felt lucky to have Miss Clark as a homeroom teacher. "Does she still pick on you?" she asked Helen.

"Not as much. Although she really blew up at me when we had to write something about Churchill."

"Why?"

"Oh, just because I asked why we always made so much fuss about people from other countries who've died. It was the same when Kennedy was shot — everyone got so dramatic about it. He wasn't *our* leader. Neither was Churchill."

Eliza was shocked. Her poem about Churchill's death had been selected for the school magazine. "But Churchill and Kennedy were great men!" she exclaimed.

Helen shrugged. "Maybe . . . Anyhow, Fitch said I was rude and selfish. But the whole class hates her now. They're all out to bug her, not just me."

In the cupboard, Helen told Eliza every outrageous thing she'd done since she'd come to boarding school. It was an impressive list; Eliza marvelled that she'd got away with so much.

Sometimes she tried to ask Helen more about her parents. The brief information she'd heard last term had become magnified in her mind. She pictured Helen's mother as being cold and heartless, and her step-father as cruel. "Is your step-father mean to you?" she asked.

"Not mean — he doesn't have enough energy for that. He's just boring. We have nothing at all in common. I don't know how my mother could have married such a totally uninteresting person after my father." Her voice became tight. "But I don't want to talk about him."

Eliza stopped quizzing her. Helen acted as if she had no family, as if Ashdown was the only world she had ever inhabited.

Although she spent a lot of time with Helen, Eliza tried not to neglect Carrie. She didn't see why the three of them couldn't all be friends. Helen didn't ski, but Carrie did; she and Eliza always stayed together on the slopes. On non-skiing Saturdays Eliza began to ask Helen, as well as Carrie, to her aunt and uncle's. But these Saturdays were always a strain. Carrie and Helen were polite to each other in public, but each voiced doubts to Eliza in private.

"I don't see why she had to come out with us," said Carrie. "She makes me nervous. I'm always afraid she's going to say something awful in front of your relatives."

"You said last term that Helen didn't bother you anymore," Eliza reminded her.

"Yes, but I never thought we'd have to be together so much. She's too crazy."

"Turps slows us down," complained Helen. "We could have stayed on the beach a lot longer if she hadn't made us bring that boring baby with us."

Eliza began to feel she was in the middle of a tug of war between her two friends. "Can't just the two of us go?" objected Carrie, when Eliza suggested that Carrie, Helen and herself watch the senior house basketball game together. "I just want *you*," insisted Helen, when Eliza began to call Carrie to join them in the group a prefect was taking over to Crabby Crump's.

One week Helen even asked if she could be Eliza's partner for church. "But I'm Carrie's!" said Eliza, before she could think of a less hurtful reply. It was an Ashdown tradition that you always had the same partner for church: either your best friend or someone like a sister or cousin or friend from home, whom you might not see much of the rest of the week but always claimed for Sundays.

There was an odd number of boarders, however, and Helen was the one left over. She usually had to walk into church with the matron, unless someone was sick. Eliza now realized how awful this must be, but she couldn't think of a solution. After her reply Helen just walked away. She never mentioned it again. Then Eliza felt angry at both of them: at Carrie for making her reject Helen, and at Helen for putting Eliza in the position of having to reject her.

Aunt Susan and Uncle Adrian went to Hawaii for ten days. Skiing had ended, and there were two Saturdays in a row when Eliza had to find someone to go out with. On the first one she was invited home by Thea Crawford.

Thea's family lived near Little Mountain, in a grey stucco house that seemed to overflow with small scruffy children and yappy dogs, although there were only two of each. Thea was undemanding and cheerful; it was a rest to be with her instead of Helen and Carrie.

They pedalled to the top of the park, then paused to get their breaths. It was an unusually dry day, and the mountains and city were spread out clearly below them. Eliza had borrowed Thea's sister's bike. It was too small for her, but riding a bike again was an intense pleasure. She longed for her own, lying neglected in the Chapmans' garage in Edmonton.

"Do you ride your bike to school?" Eliza asked Thea.

"I take the bus. There's no prefects on our route, so we have a great time. We try to land our berets on each other's heads. The bus driver gets pretty mad."

"I wish I was a day-girl," said Eliza enviously.

"Oh, but I wish I was a boarder! From what you say it sounds like so much fun."

"It isn't this term."

"You make lifelong friends in boarding school, though," said Thea earnestly. "That's what my mother says. Is Carrie your best friend?"

"Carrie and Helen."

"Helen? Really? She's so . . ." Thea paused.

Eliza looked at her defiantly. "She's *nice*. I really like her."

"Oh, I'm sure she is, if you say so," said Thea hastily. "Come on, let's go and see what's for dinner. Coasting back's the best part."

The next week Carrie invited Eliza out with her and her parents, who were coming up from Seattle for the weekend. Eliza knew that Linda O.'s parents were also in town, and had asked Helen to join them for the day.

"I think I'll stay in," said Eliza. "I have some prep to do." She didn't, but the prospect of having a day alone tempted her. And she had never remained at the school on a Saturday before; she was curious to see what it was like.

On Friday Helen was gleeful because she'd received a twenty-dollar bill in the mail from her grandmother in Montreal. She snapped it between her fingers. "Boy oh boy, do I need this!" she crowed, as she and Eliza struggled out of the crowd surrounding the mail slots.

"Why did she send it?" asked Eliza. "And isn't it risky not to send a cheque?"

"It's a late Christmas present," said Helen quickly. "She always sends me twenty dollars, but this year she forgot, so I wrote and reminded her. She's getting pretty doddery — that's probably why she sent cash."

"Are you going to buy something with it tomorrow?"

"Oh, I think I'll save it. You never know when it might come in handy. I'll take it down to the office later." She pocketed the money and walked away, whistling merrily.

Helen had changed. Last term she would have spent the money immediately on food. There was something odd about her behaviour, something Eliza couldn't pin down.

On Saturday morning Eliza sat on the stairs, watching the stream of people arrive to sign out the other boarders. It felt queer not to be going out herself. When she said hello to Carrie's parents they repeated their invitation and she almost gave in. But after everyone had left she tramped all over the main floor of the residence with relish. She'd never been so alone in it before; the old building creaked in welcome. Snuggling into a chair in the Blue Sitting Room, she began to make up a story about a family who had lived in the house before it became a school. The misty rain outside made the room seem even cosier. Eliza sighed contentedly: it was so peaceful to sit still and do absolutely nothing.

Only six other boarders were staying in this week: three grade nines, two grade tens, and one grade twelve. Mrs Renfrew found Eliza and said she was taking them all up to Oakridge to shop.

"I think I'd rather stay here," said Eliza.

"Well, you can't," said the Pouncer gruffly. "Miss Tavistock is out for the morning and there's no one else in the residence."

"But Margaret's staying." Eliza had seen the older girl go over to the school with her books.

"Margaret is seventeen. You are only twelve. Now get your coat, Eliza, and stop arguing."

The matron let them loose in Woodward's while she did her own shopping, with instructions to meet her in an hour at the White Spot. "Be sure to stay together — Judith and Gail, you're in charge."

First they looked at records. While Frances was buying one, Eliza managed to escape into the stationery department nearby. She pecked experimentally on a demonstration typewriter:

Eliza Chapman
Elizabeth Chapman
Elizabeth Norah Chapman
Elizabeth N. Chapman
E. Norah Chapman
E.N. Chapman
E.N.C.

Gail found her there and made her come back. Then they pushed into a cubicle while Patti tried on a new bra — all except Eliza, who refused to go in. She wondered if they knew she didn't wear one yet.

For the last fifteen minutes the six of them stood at the cosmetics counter, spraying perfume samples on their wrists and trying on make-up. Eliza got bored with this very quickly. She wanted to go to the library in the mall, but the others wouldn't let her. "Come on, Eliza, let's put some blusher on you," said Patti.

"Stop it!" Eliza squirmed out of the way of the advancing brush loaded with red powder. She examined some lipsticks sullenly. They were all acting so silly; she would *never* be like this.

When they got back to school, Barbara asked Eliza if she wanted to listen to their new record with them in the Rose Sitting Room. "We'll teach you the Jerk," she offered.

"No thanks," said Eliza. "I'm going for a walk."

It was still drizzling, but she changed into her jeans and ski jacket, put her hood up and went out. Wandering slowly through the grounds, she felt the same affection for the physical beauty of Ashdown that she had in the first term. It wasn't the school that was the problem; it was her. If her family lived in Vancouver she'd still want to come here.

The air smelled like clean dirt. Even though it was only the end of February, yellow forsythia blossoms were already brightening the woods by the playing field, and jewel-coloured crocuses were poking their heads up by the swings. Eliza rubbed a shiny green bud between her fingers. In Edmonton and Toronto there would still be snow on the ground.

Up in her favourite tree, she sat on a branch and swung her legs, humming an odd little song they'd learned in choir that week: "I care for nobody, no! not I/ If nobody cares for me." At the moment the words seemed true; she didn't want to be with anyone but herself.

An hour later, however, she began to get restless. She was back in the Blue Sitting Room with a book, but she'd read it twice already. If only she'd been able to get to the public library — now she couldn't go until the walk on Wednesday. And she had gone through all the interesting-looking books in the school library.

Beatle music blared cheerfully through the wall of the Rose Sitting Room next door. Eliza liked the Beatles, but not when she was trying to read. And Mrs

Renfrew, who seemed to think Eliza was about three, had forbidden her to go into the dorm: "You'll just mess it up in there."

The music became shriller, overpowering the ticking hall clock. What could she do for the rest of the afternoon? Turn on the TV, but there wouldn't be anything good on at this time of day. Practise or study, but she'd done both this morning; and, after all, it was Saturday, not a school day. Eliza sighed. She wondered what Carrie and Helen were doing.

Then she heard Miss Tavistock's voice in the hall. "Yes, I know you need it loud for dancing, but it's *too* loud . . . no, lower still . . . that's better." The head-mistress put her head in at the door of the Blue Sitting Room. "Are you busy, Elizabeth?"

Eliza stood up hastily, her book sliding to the floor. "Um . . . no, not exactly, Miss Tavistock."

"I'm going to visit my aunt — would you like to come?"

"Do you mean Miss Peck?" Eliza had never seen the school founder, a very old lady who came to the school only once a year, to the School Birthday in April.

"Yes . . . I visit her every Saturday. She enjoys meeting the younger students."

"Oh, yes please," said Eliza, glad of a novelty.

"Very well, go up and put on a skirt and I'll meet you in the hall in five minutes."

Miss Tavistock drove a neat little grey Austin, which she zipped efficiently through the Saturday traffic as Eliza sat tongue-tied beside her.

"You seem to be having a rather gloomy term, Elizabeth," said Miss Tavistock, continuing down Forty-First Avenue after she'd manoeuvred the bottleneck of cars in Kerrisdale.

Why did everyone have to notice that? Eliza didn't answer. It was unfair of Miss Tavistock to pin her down when she was in a car and couldn't get away; and it hadn't been a question anyway. There was a long, uncomfortable silence. The car's tires hissed on the wet pavement.

"I hope you would come and tell me if something was really bothering you," said the headmistress finally. "Would you?"

This did require an answer. "Yes, Miss Tavistock," murmured Eliza, relieved that they'd turned into a driveway leading to a low white building. The sign in front read "Crestwood Retirement Home."

The hall was suffocatingly warm. White-haired heads bent over cards or stared pensively at a large television, but they looked alertly at Eliza as she and Miss Tavistock passed them. "Look — a child!" she heard one woman whisper to her neighbour. Many of them nodded and said hello. Eliza was embarrassed to cause such a fuss, and she was relieved when they reached Miss Peck's door.

"Come in," a fluty voice called in answer to their knock. An upright, brittle-looking figure sat in an armchair by the window. Miss Peck had a red tartan blanket draped over her knees and was beating time to a stirring march on the radio. The room was much too small for all the heavy furniture crammed into it.

"I've brought someone to see you, Aunt Dora. This is Elizabeth Chapman, one of our grade seven boarders. Elizabeth, this is Miss Peck."

"How delightful!" said the old lady, leaning forward to turn down the radio. She had a precise English accent. "Come closer, my dear, and let me touch you."

Miss Tavistock had said her aunt was nearly blind, but Eliza hadn't been prepared for this. She walked over and shook a hand that felt like a few sticks in a soft skin bag. She whispered a "How do you do."

Miss Peck was much like her portrait in Miss Tavistock's study, but the real woman was older, thinner and friendlier. Eliza remembered trying to make the mouth in the painting turn upwards. This face was all wrinkly smiles.

"How cold your hands are! Sit down here beside me and we'll get some hot tea inside you. What does she look like, Charlotte?"

"She's tall for her age and has short, light brown hair and greyish-blue eyes. Although your hair is beginning to fall *into* your eyes, Elizabeth. We'll have to get it cut soon."

Miss Tavistock plugged in an electric kettle she'd filled in the bathroom and got teacups from a corner cupboard. How strange to hear her called Charlotte! The aunt and niece looked remarkably alike, except for the older woman's fuzzy white halo of hair with pink patches showing through it.

"Where do you come from, Elizabeth? How do you like boarding?" Miss Peck listened intently to Eliza's answers as Miss Tavistock handed their tea to them and opened a package of Jaffa Cakes she had brought.

It was difficult to look at someone you were speaking to when that person couldn't see you back. It seemed rude. Eliza forgot to be shy, however, as she described her family and the school, and she forgot to be homesick as she tried to make both subjects interesting for her listener. It was hard to believe that this frail person had started Ashdown. "What was it like when it first opened?" Eliza asked.

Miss Peck's wavering voice strengthened as she told Eliza how the school had begun with only six students coming to lessons in a house downtown, about the long black skirts they had worn and about the move to the present property. "It's called Ashdown after Ashdown Forest in England, where I lived as a child. That's where Winnie-the-Pooh is from, you know," she added with a twinkle. "You look at the illustrations in the books — that's Ashdown Forest." Eliza promised she would, although she felt much too old for Winnie-the-Pooh.

"Of course I was a child long before Pooh came into existence. I'm a Victorian, my dear — what do you think of that?"

"Don't be absurd, Aunt Dora," said Miss Tavistock fondly. "You're much more modern than I am."

The two of them showed Eliza a scrapbook about the school through the years. For the first time since December, Eliza felt proud to be an Ashdown student. She watched Miss Peck as she and her niece discussed members of their family. It must have taken a lot of courage to start your own school.

"How old is she?" she asked Miss Tavistock on their way back in the car.

"Ninety-three. Isn't she amazing? She was my model when I was a young girl in Victoria. I wanted to be exactly like her." Eliza asked the headmistress about her early teaching days, relieved the two of them could talk comfortably again.

"I saw Miss Peck," said Eliza casually that night.

Helen's head popped out of her pyjama jacket; she never unbuttoned it and was always getting stuck. "Poor you. Were you dragged to tea? I've been three times. Now I make sure I'm out of sight on Saturday afternoons."

"I *liked* her. She's really interesting. She told me all about starting the school."

Pam yawned. "She tells us that every year on the School Birthday. She's sweet, but kind of boring."

"She's not boring at all," said Eliza in a low voice, but only to John under the covers.

"I wish you'd been with us today, Eliza," said Carrie. "We went to Capilano Canyon and walked on the suspension bridge. It was scary!"

"I *liked* staying in." Eliza knew she was being unfriendly, but she didn't care. She rolled over and pretended she was an early Ashdown student. She would wear a black dress and a white pinafore, with long black stockings and buttoned boots — or did they wear shoes then? They would all sit in a circle, learning lessons around the fire . . .

XII

In the Sickroom

As soon as the bell rang on March 1, Pam shouted "Rabbits!" For good luck, you were supposed to say "Hares!" last thing at night at the end of the month and "Rabbits!" first thing the next morning. Eliza hadn't remembered once; Pam or Carrie always did. Every time she forgot she wondered if she would be unlucky that day.

But this morning began with a good omen. Carrie picked a thread off Eliza's blazer. "You're going to get a letter," she said, stretching it out between her hands. "A long one!" And sure enough, after lunch Eliza snatched a fat envelope out of the "C" pigeonhole.

It was from her mother. Alone in the dorm, she started reading it, then wished she hadn't.

She was not to go to Toronto for Easter because her parents were going to a conference in Halifax for most of the April holiday. "The twins are staying with your grandparents," wrote her mother, "but you can come with us if you really want to. It's a long and expensive trip, however, and I really think you'd have more fun at Harrison Hot Springs with Susan and Adrian. You've never been there and you'd love it."

I've never been to Halifax either, thought Eliza furiously, although Halifax had nothing to do with it. It was not seeing them in a month that was the blow. She knew she was being unfair. It was very expensive to send her away to school in the first place, and plane fares all the way to the other coast of Canada made it much worse.

"If you weren't so happy there we wouldn't even suggest you not coming, sweetheart," continued the letter. "But June isn't very far away. Please let us know what you think."

Eliza stopped reading the rest of her mother's usual lengthy news. June was *years* away. She'd never last that long. She wished she could explode in loud wails, but she was too hurt and angry to even cry. They seemed to think she was exactly the same person she'd been at Christmas, excited and happy about being at Ashdown.

But of course she'd given them no reason to think otherwise. She couldn't change that now and make them fly her to Halifax like a spoiled child. It wasn't the way she liked to think of herself.

That night she wrote back and said of course she didn't mind. The person who wrote the letter seemed like someone else. And the heaviness inside her, which had just begun to lighten lately, increased until she felt immobilized by misery.

The next morning she opened her eyes and remembered: she wasn't going home for Easter. Then she didn't want to get out of bed.

"What's the matter with you, Eliza?" asked Carrie at lunch. "You're so quiet."

Eliza just shrugged. She couldn't speak to anyone; it was too much of a struggle just to get through the day. The feeling of not being able to cope was terrifying.

In art, the last period of the afternoon, Eliza took her ball of clay over to a corner by herself and tried to model a horse. It would be the Black Stallion; she wished she could ride him out of here. But as soon as she stood the horse up on its spindly legs, it collapsed into a grey heap and its head fell off.

She began again by throwing the clay down hard on her board to get rid of the air bubbles. *Thwack! Thwack!* That made her feel a tiny bit better. THWACK! Miss Macdonald frowned at her from across the room: "I think you've done enough of that, Elizabeth."

As Eliza bent over the flattened lump of clay she suddenly felt dizzy, and a terrible trickle welling up in her mouth warned her she was about to be sick. Pressing her lips tightly together, she rushed from the Art Room into the bathroom outside the door.

When it was over, she turned helplessly to Miss Macdonald, who had followed her out. "All right,

Elizabeth?" The teacher handed Eliza a paper cup of water to rinse out her mouth and a piece of toilet paper to blow her nose. "Can you make it over to the sickroom now? Are you finished?"

"I think so," whispered Eliza, hoping it was true.

Thea was delegated to take her over. She put her arms around Eliza's shoulders as they walked across the driveway. "You poor thing — it's awful to barf," she said cheerfully. "But I bet it will be fun, being in the sickroom."

It didn't feel like fun at all. Eliza watched her body being bundled into one of the hard narrow beds by Miss Monaghan. The nurse put a basin and a towel by the bed and then left her alone. Eliza closed her eyes and sank at once into sleep. The last sound she heard was the juniors playing outside the window:

Red Rover, Red Rover
We call Janie over.

Their high voices turned into a dream. Her parents were on one side of a field, lined up with the Demons, her Toronto grandparents and her friends from Edmonton. She was on the other side, among a group of shadowy Ashdown students.

Red Rover, Red Rover
We call Eliza over

called her mother and father.

She couldn't move. "Let me go!" she sobbed, struggling with the strong hands that gripped each of

her arms. "Let me go!" They relaxed their hold and she
was free. She looked across to her family and friends.

Red Rover, Red Rover
We call Eliza over

they chanted again. But now their faces looked
greedy, as if, when she reached them, they would
hold her just as tightly as the students had.

"No!" shouted Eliza, and she ran away between
the two lines — away from them all.

She woke up shivering. There was no more chanting
outside the window. The curtains had been drawn
and the room was dim.

"Are you feeling better, Eliza?" asked a small,
friendly voice. Eliza turned her head and realized
there were three other people in the sickroom.

The voice belonged to Holly, the youngest
boarder, who was only nine. Her bright eyes examined Eliza with interest from the next bed. In the
other two beds were Maureen, in grade eight, and
Beth, in grade eleven.

"Eliza might not feel like talking, Holly," said
Beth softly, "and Maureen's asleep. Why don't you
read your comic?"

Holly opened it up obediently, but she kept staring at Eliza over the top of it.

You can't even be sick in peace here, thought
Eliza. She had never wanted to go home so much. She
longed for her own blue-and-white room in Edmon-

ton, with her mother there to take care of her. All at once she sat up and vomited again into the basin. Then she lay back weakly against the pillow, tears sliding over her hot cheeks.

Miss Monaghan was at her side in an instant. "Poor Eliza," she clucked, as she cleaned her up. "Are you feeling terrible, then? It's a bad bug, this flue, but you'll be rid of it in a few days. Now don't *cry*, pet! Don't cry . . ." She held Eliza's shaking shoulders, smoothed back her hair and tucked the blankets firmly around her. Eliza drifted off again, pretending the cool hand on her forehead was her mother's. This time she dreamed she was being rocked; and then the gentle rocking transported her into a bottomless sleep with no dreams at all.

The next morning she woke up automatically just before the rising bell clanged outside the door. She looked around with surprise at the pristine white room, the brown woolly curtains with bright sunlight glinting through their cracks and the three sleeping forms beside her. I'm in the sickroom, she thought, stretching luxuriously. I don't have to get up at all. She felt perfectly all right. Not nauseated anymore, and strangely airy inside; better, in fact, than she'd felt all term.

Lazily she watched Holly wake up. The little girl's eyes popped open, and she sat up at once and began talking. "I threw up in the night, Eliza — did you hear me?"

Eliza wrinkled her nose. "No, but I can smell it!"

The nurse came in as the other two were stirring. "Now, how are you all today?"

Holly told her in great detail how she'd been sick, proudly showing Miss Monaghan the evidence in her basin.

"You should have pressed the buzzer for me, Holly — that's what it's for." It was odd how much more Matilda focused on you when she was a nurse than when she was a matron. In the dorms she was vague, but in the sickroom she was all solicitous attention.

Beth said she felt feverish, and Miss Monaghan stuck a thermometer into her mouth. Maureen thought she was better. "Well, stay in bed until noon, and we'll see. You can leave then if you're all right. How are *you*, Eliza?"

Eliza thought fast. "I was sick in the night, too," she lied. "But I made it to the bathroom. I think I *could* be sick again."

"You keep still and warm, and I'll bring you some ginger ale. Maureen, you may have a light breakfast — I'll just nip out and order it."

Eliza was ravenous after no dinner the night before. Her mouth watered as she watched Maureen eat a boiled egg, and she sipped her tepid ginger ale slowly, trying to make it last.

Except that she felt hungry, the rest of the morning passed pleasantly. It was sinfully delicious to stay in bed and listen to the clatter of the boarders' feet as they hurried down to breakfast. After they left for classes the residence was silent except for the distant ticking of the hall clock, the whine of a vacuum cleaner upstairs and the drone of a plane tracing a path against the blue sky. Eliza even began to think it was better than being sick at home; here there was lots of company.

Beth didn't talk much, for which Eliza was grateful. She was Madeline's best friend, and Eliza felt shy with her. Maureen, a notorious gossip from the Red Dorm, informed Eliza about all the grade eight daygirls. Most of their attention, however, was absorbed by Holly.

Everyone liked her. She came from a logging camp far up on Vancouver Island, where there were no schools. She was small, neat and self-contained, calmly accepting the fuss everyone always made over her. Helen had been the same age when she came to Ashdown, and Eliza wondered if she had adapted as easily as Holly had. It wasn't very likely.

Eliza couldn't imagine herself living away from home at age nine. Yet Holly didn't seem homesick at all, and Eliza felt ashamed of her own recent unhappiness.

She and Maureen took turns reading aloud *Struwwelpeter,* which they found on a shelf of old books. It was so ridiculously gruesome they had a hard time speaking through their laughter. Even Beth seemed to enjoy it. But Holly didn't laugh; she listened gravely, her eyes wide.

Maureen left at noon, and while Holly and Beth slept, Eliza read two more of the books. One was an English school story, like the ones she had at home. As she read it, she thought about how different Ash-

down really was from a story. The nice parts were just
as good, but the bad parts were worse, and the books
said nothing about all the dull parts in between. Being
sick, however, was turning into a good part. She felt
totally relaxed, with nothing to worry about. Except
for being hungry.

"I think I could manage to eat something now,"
she told Miss Monaghan later that afternoon. She
could hear the boarders at tea and drooled at the
thought of the huge oatmeal cookies they always had.

"You haven't been sick all day — how about
some chicken broth?"

That was better than nothing. Eliza slurped it up
eagerly; she had never tasted anything so good. "I
don't know how you can eat," shuddered Beth and
Holly, who had both been sick again.

In the evening the nurse brought in the television
and they lay back comfortably against their pillows
and watched it. Their lights were turned out at eight
o'clock, but Eliza wasn't tired. She stayed awake for
a long time, trying to figure out how she could spend
at least one more day in the sickroom.

It stretched out to two. Eliza discovered that if she just
said she *felt* sick she was allowed to have dry toast,
soup, ginger ale and tea, "to see if you can keep it
down." The other two were beginning to feel better
and had some food too, but they couldn't swallow
more than a few mouthfuls. When they weren't looking, Eliza stole the pieces of toast they left on their
trays, hid them under her pillow and gulped them
down at night.

The two-day space became a special little world, inhabited only by Beth, Holly and herself. Miss Monaghan left them alone for long periods, since she still had to look after the juniors upstairs.

They spent the whole of Thursday morning cutting out Holly's book of paper dolls. Holly was the neatest cutter, but she was used to it. Eliza was amazed how much she enjoyed folding back the white tabs and fitting the clothes carefully onto the cardboard figures. Her fingers remembered the pleasure of it from years ago.

"This is really fun!" said Beth, slitting open a hat. She was a quiet girl, with a serious face. Eliza knew she wrote poetry; it was often published in the school magazine. It surprised her that Beth was helping them with the dolls. Somehow the three of them all seemed the same age.

They named the dolls — Prudence, Marigold, Amaryllis and Rose — and had a fashion parade across Holly's bed. Then they played Battleships and Hangman, made up elephant jokes and told ghost stories.

That evening a large parcel arrived for Eliza. It contained schoolbooks, some of her own books, Helen's radio and John. There was a note inside:

Dear Eliza,
Miss Clark made Pam send your homework. We were going to put in food, but then we remembered why you went in there! We thought you would be missing your bear. Get well soon!

Love,
Carrie, Helen, Pam and Jean

It was too bad about the food, but Eliza was touched. She missed the others; it felt like more than two days since she had seen them. She knew John was supposed to be a joke, but she was delighted to have him. They made him a paper hat, and Eliza let Holly keep him on her bed. She shoved her homework under her own bed; she would just tell her teachers she hadn't felt well enough to concentrate.

"Madeline's told me a lot about you," said Beth on Friday morning, when Holly was taking a bath. "She thinks you'll be a prefect one day, you're so enthusiastic."

Eliza was flabbergasted. A prefect! And she certainly hadn't been enthusiastic this term. Her cheeks turned pink with surprised pleasure. Since the week of her dare she had avoided Madeline, but it appeared that Madeline had not forgotten her, after all.

"I could never be a prefect," she said shyly. "I won't be here then."

"Aren't you at Ashdown until grade twelve?"

"Oh no — just this year." Imagine boarding for five more years! Although most girls stayed, once they'd started. Everyone else in the Yellow Dorm would be here that long. Eliza remembered that her parents had once considered sending her in grade ten — what if they still did? The possibility put a new light on everything, but she didn't want to think of it right now.

She would much rather talk more about her house captain. "Do you think Madeline will be head girl next year?" she asked Beth.

"Lots of people do. I'm not sure she wants to — she's worried enough about having time for her music when she's a prefect, which she's sure to be, of course. And . . . well, she may have other plans for next year."

"*What* other plans?"

But Beth acted as if she'd already said too much about her friend. Eliza was too exhilarated by Madeline's high expectations of her to worry about it. She felt ashamed for neglecting Madeline; perhaps if they became close again the other girl would tell whatever she was being so mysterious about.

Eliza wondered if Beth wanted to be a prefect. It was supposed to be such an honour. Pam had already informed Eliza that *she* intended to be elected one, which was why she was always trying to make such an impression. Eliza couldn't, and didn't want to, imagine being old enough to wear a light blue blazer and boss everyone else around.

Holly returned and they had strenuous races with some crutches they found in a cupboard. Miss Monaghan appeared and stopped them. "I think all of you are better! But you may as well stay in here today, since it's Friday. Then you'll be rested for school next week."

She finally gave them some real food: egg sandwiches and carrot sticks and applesauce. As Eliza gobbled it up she knew she would be ready to leave tomorrow, thinking with relish of the good dinners she always got at Aunt Susan's.

That evening Eliza crept to the door and listened to

evening prayers being conducted on the other side of the wall. She was beginning to wonder what had been happening in the residence while she'd been away.

Miss Tavistock cleared her throat and began her nightly talk. Usually it only consisted of trivial announcements, but this evening she had a longer speech. "I am happy to be able to tell you that whoever has been taking money from the Pound Box has returned it. I'm still sorry that this person has not had the courage to confess, but I would like to thank whoever it is for paying the money back. I hope she has learned her lesson and will never do such a thing again. That's all I wish to say about the matter — we'll consider it closed."

"What did she say?" asked Holly, when Eliza had got back into bed.

"Oh, nothing much. I couldn't really hear."

She escaped into a book for the rest of the evening. But after Lights Out she had to face the revelation she'd had while listening to the headmistress's words.

It was Helen. She was the thief. All sorts of niggling suspicions that had prodded Eliza's mind during the term came together in this certainty. She remembered the licorice Helen had bought for the feast — and the radio. And the money she'd given Miss Bixley for the cake. But the most glaring evidence was the twenty-dollar bill Helen had asked for from her grandmother — she must have felt really desperate. That's what she used to pay it back, and that's why she'd been so cheerful that day: she'd been relieved.

She also must have been scared, after Miss Tavistock's lecture in January. That explained why Helen was so full of nervous energy this term, and why she seemed to be harbouring a secret. Eliza couldn't imagine how she had managed the interview with Miss Tavistock, but Helen had always been a good actor.

It was wrong to steal, of course, although she *had* paid it back. What worried Eliza more was the amount of trouble her friend could have got into by risking so much. But what bothered her the most was that Helen hadn't told her. Eliza felt cheated, as if the person she had thought she knew all along had turned into someone else.

Now she even wondered if Helen had been stealing, after all, when she was younger. She felt guilty about not believing her. But what if Helen had told her she was innocent so Eliza would feel sorry for her and be her friend? I would have been friends with her anyway, she thought.

But would she? She hadn't known Helen very well then. It wouldn't have been much of a draw to friendship, to admit you were a thief.

Now she had to know. She had to talk to Helen about it. It all had to come out into the open, or they couldn't keep on being friends.

Although she was sorry to end her peaceful time there, she could hardly wait to get out of the sickroom. Beth and Holly seemed like sisters, but Eliza knew that would end when they were all back in their dorms.

When Eliza walked into the Yellow Dorm after breakfast the next morning she was greeted with hoots of delight. She grinned at them all, but reddened at the sight of Helen.

"Helen lost *two* house points for fooling around in the play rehearsal," said Pam. Helen shrugged proudly.

"I got my perm all cut off — see, Eliza?" said Jean, whirling around for approval.

Carrie pulled Eliza over to her bed. "I have something to ask you. Are you going to Toronto for Easter? If you aren't, would you like to come home with me? My parents would love to have you."

Eliza felt a bubble of anticipation rise up inside her. It would be much more interesting to visit Carrie in Seattle than to stay in a hotel at Harrison Hot Springs and help look after the baby. She had never been to the United States before. "Oh, yes," she said eagerly. "I'd like to, Carrie. I'll ask my parents."

She didn't have to think of a way to talk to Helen; the latter did it for her. "Let's meet in the cape cupboard tomorrow after rest," she whispered. "I have lots to tell you."

XIII

Helen Confesses

For the rest of the weekend Eliza hoped that Helen was going to tell her everything herself. But the other girl had had nothing specific in mind. They sat in the cupboard on Sunday afternoon and Eliza listened to her chatter about the school play. She worked up the courage to speak, glad it was so dark in the cupboard and that she didn't have to see Helen's face.

"You aren't even listening," complained Helen, when Eliza failed to laugh at her latest remark.

"No, because I have to ask you something." Eliza took a deep breath. "Did you take the Pound Money?"

There was total silence. Now Eliza wished that she *could* see Helen's face, and that she hadn't sounded so accusing. "I just have to know, Helen, that's all," she added pleadingly.

"Yup . . . I took it. I'm the thief. Now I suppose you don't like me any more. Although I was only borrowing it, you know. I meant to pay it back all along, and I didn't think they'd find out so soon. They don't usually open up the box until the end of the year."

"You could have been expelled or something. Weren't you scared when they found out?"

"Well, sort of." This much of an admission of fear from Helen meant she'd been really frightened. "But I stopped taking it before Christmas. I decided I never would again, and I won't. Do you believe me?" Helen's voice was savage, but Eliza knew by now that she sounded angriest when she really cared about something.

"I *would* believe you," Eliza began slowly, "except for one thing." This was the hardest part. "Did you lie to me about stealing in Prince George? You didn't have to, you know."

Helen thumped the floor of the cupboard with her fist. "I didn't lie to you! I didn't steal then, I told you that! It just kind of gave me the idea for doing it last term, and for doing it . . ." She stopped.

And for doing it before that? Eliza almost said aloud, but she silenced herself just in time — it was too much like a question Pam would ask. And she didn't want to hear any more. What other secret was Helen going to reveal? She seemed more of a stranger every second.

Helen finally answered anyhow. "Listen, Eliza," she said fiercely, leaning over and clutching Eliza's shoulders. This was unusual; Helen never touched people. "Listen very carefully, because I never want to talk about this again. When I first came to Ashdown I *felt* like a thief. My mother drilled it into me the whole time I was waiting to come here. So I took little things — mostly food from the kitchen or the tuck boxes, or people's china animals or comics, which I returned later. I just wanted to see if I could do it — it relieved the boredom. I didn't take any money until this year. It was *borrowing,* not stealing," she added, as if trying to convince herself.

"But why did you?" Eliza asked curiously. "You didn't need it. You get pocket money like the rest of us."

"I *did* need it! I had no pocket money left the week we had the feast, and that was my idea, so I had to bring something. And then it was beginning to look like an awful term. Fidget was bugging me, and you guys were so busy being good. I had to have the radio, just to keep from cracking up. I was going to stop after that, but everyone gets their family to send them a birthday cake, or at least gets the money for one. But my stingy parents wouldn't give me any because my marks were so low."

"Didn't you get *anything* for your birthday?"

"Underwear. What a lousy present. So I took some money one more time. I was surprised there was enough left, but the Pouncer makes a pile out of all of us. It was just those three times, though. I never will again. And I *never* stole with those kids. I had no idea what they were doing. Now do you believe me?"

Eliza knew their friendship hung on her answer.

She wanted so badly to trust Helen that she did, even though she still felt shaken by this new revelation about her.

"I believe you," she breathed. "I wish you'd told me about the Pound Money. I could have helped you pay it back. But I suppose it was none of my business. I do believe you, and I'm sorry I asked."

"Do you promise you'll never tell?"

"Of course I won't!" cried Eliza. "You know that!"

Helen jumped up. "Let's go out and swing. It's not raining. Why are we wasting our time in here?"

March seemed to speed by, and Eliza felt so much better she could hardly remember how miserable she'd been. Her homesickness had melted down to a small, manageable ache. She began to seek out Madeline again and the older girl seemed glad of her company, although she was as preoccupied as ever. Best of all, Eliza was still friends with Helen.

After the spell in the sickroom she felt whole again, as if she had recovered from a much longer illness than a pretend flu. The weeks of gloomy rain had ended. Every day the Yellow Dorm spent as much time as possible outside. Later, as they lay in bed and talked, they could still smell the sweet spring air through the open windows.

Sometimes their talks lasted long into the night, especially because they so often turned into a debate. This happened the evening they argued about God.

It started with Carrie asking what religion everyone was outside of school. Her family was Lutheran, and Jean's was Presbyterian. Helen didn't know. "I guess I was baptized," she said, "although I don't remember, of course. My grandmother's Catholic and she's always saying I should be too, but you won't catch *me* joining a church. We get too much of it here."

Eliza and Pam were the only ones who went to an Anglican church at home as well as at school. "I don't believe in God, though," said Pam bluntly.

Jean looked shocked. "Don't believe in God!"

"Me neither," said Helen. She and Pam exchanged a surprised glance; it was so rare that they agreed on anything.

"*I* do," said Carrie calmly. "I don't see any reason not to."

Eliza was stunned. Pam's flat statement had swept through her like a cold wind. And what a hypocrite she was, if she didn't believe — she always wrote flowery essays about God for scripture class.

"Put it this way," continued Pam. "It's like saying to someone, 'There's an orange behind that bush,' and they have to believe you without being allowed to look. It just doesn't make sense."

"But that's the whole point!" Jean's voice was trembling but determined. "Believing there *is,* without knowing, means you have to have faith!" She looked to Eliza for support. "What about *you,* Eliza? You believe in God, don't you?"

"I guess so." Eliza shifted in her bunk guiltily. She had always thought she did, so why couldn't she answer more confidently? This was probably going to be one of those questions it was going to take years to figure out — like so many other things this term.

"Why don't *you*, Helen?" persisted Jean, after giving Eliza a puzzled look.

Helen yawned. "I've never seen any use for it. Though if you want to, Scotty, carry on," she added, unusually gentle, as she always was with Jean. Then she became fierce. "But I sure know there's no Santa Claus up in the sky to grant you wishes."

Eliza wondered, as she often had lately, how much Helen had suffered in her life. At the moment she seemed like the oldest, not the youngest, in the Yellow Dorm.

Then Jean started arguing with Pam, becoming more and more agitated. Pam seemed just as bothered that Jean was disagreeing with her for once as she was by what Jean was saying. Carrie defended Jean staunchly, and Helen occasionally added an argument on Pam's side. Eliza just listened, her mind in a whirl.

When Jean came close to tears, however, they knew it was time to stop. "I don't see why we have to talk about it so much," concluded Carrie firmly. "You either believe in God or you don't, and I do." She got up and closed the curtains, giving Jean a reassuring smile.

How different we all are, thought Eliza in the dark silence that still rang with words. But the others, unlike her, were at least *certain* about their differences. She felt so wishy-washy. If she really believed in God, for instance, she should probably condemn Helen's stealing. If she didn't, then maybe it shouldn't bother her. But she always found herself wavering, and then, because she didn't want to think any less of her friend, she just told herself it was Helen's problem, not hers.

She lifted the curtain and looked out at the clear cold stars. Where did they come from? Nobody knew. For some reason that was a comforting thought. If nobody knew, then she didn't have to.

A week later, Helen's parents arrived in Vancouver.

"The brat needs glasses and they want to get a second opinion," Helen explained to Eliza, scowling. "My mother can't stand the idea of another daughter in specs."

They were only coming for one day, and Helen was to join them for dinner. The only time you could go out on a weekday was when your parents were in town.

"Why don't you ask me too?" said Eliza. The thought of meeting Helen's parents was scary, but curiosity overcame her fear. You learned a lot about people when you met their parents, and Eliza had met everyone's except Pam's and Helen's. It wasn't hard to picture Pam's — they sounded a lot like her. But Helen's mother and step-father were a mystery. It would be a pleasant surprise if they weren't as bad as Helen made them out to be.

Helen looked puzzled at her suggestion. "Do you really want to? And meet my bratty sister too? You won't have a good time."

Eliza assured her that she did. Neither Helen's

parents nor Miss Tavistock objected, so at seven on Wednesday evening she found herself sitting in a Chinese restaurant with Helen and her family.

Already she wished she hadn't come. Four-year-old Tracy kept kicking her under the table. She banged her chopsticks on her plate, refused to eat anything but rice and whined about her new glasses.

"I hate them!" she pouted, pulling them off her face and slamming them on the table. "They're ugly!"

Helen pushed up her own glasses and stared haughtily through them at her sister.

"I know they're ugly, sweetie," said Helen's mother. She put the glasses into her purse. "You can take them off for a while."

"Now Peg," objected Helen's step-father. "Dr Andrews agreed with the doctor in Prince George — she should wear them all the time. Give them back to her."

"Don't tell me what to do!" snapped his wife. They began to exchange angry, sarcastic remarks, Tracy interrupting the sharp voices with demands for ice cream.

Eliza and Helen shovelled down almond chicken in silence. Helen's face was bent so close to her plate Eliza could see only the top of her head. Never before had Eliza heard two adults attack each other so viciously. She sat stiffly, trying to pretend she was invisible.

"Everyone's listening to you," Helen muttered at last. Her mother glared at her, but the argument subsided. For the rest of the meal all the attention was focused on Tracy. Neither of her parents said anything to Helen, except to criticize her last report card. The only thing they said to Eliza was a question about where she came from.

Tracy and her father waited in the car while Helen's mother took them into the residence. She pecked her daughter's cheek. "We'll see you at Easter, Helen. I hope you're behaving yourself."

After she left, Eliza and Helen stood awkwardly in the hall. Eliza wanted desperately to say something sympathetic, but you couldn't criticize someone else's parents unless they did it first.

"Well," said Helen, shrugging. "Now you know. I wasn't exaggerating, was I?"

Quickly, before she had time to feel self-conscious, Eliza squeezed Helen's hand. Then the two of them trudged up the stairs to bed.

XIV

A New Boarder

There were two events left in the second term: the School Play and the School Birthday. Helen was the only member of the Yellow Dorm in the play, and that was an accident. One evening on the veranda she'd been demonstrating to Eliza and Carrie how Fidget, who was plump, tried to pull up her girdle in class when she thought they weren't looking. Helen tugged and squirmed and panted, not noticing when the others suddenly quenched their laughter. Miss Tavistock had come up behind her and was watching her gyrations.

"That will do, Helen," she said crisply after a few seconds. "Since you enjoy making a spectacle of yourself, perhaps you should try out for the play."

"But I couldn't be in a play, Miss Tavistock!"

"Nevertheless, I expect to hear that you attended the auditions."

Since this was clearly an order, Helen had no choice. And although she grumbled about it, she seemed pleased when she was chosen, especially since Pam, who had also auditioned, hadn't been.

The play was a musical — *Oliver!* Her dormmates had heard Helen rehearse the songs so often that they knew them all by heart. On opening night they sat with Eliza's aunt and uncle and Jean's parents, watching her proudly.

Helen was one of the street urchins. With torn knickers, bare feet, burnt cork smudged across her face and her hair sticking straight up with exertion, she looked just like a mischievous boy. She had no lines, but as she cavorted around the stage with the rest of Fagin's Gang, Eliza marvelled at her intense involvement. It wasn't like Helen to get caught up in school activities.

"Watch out for pickpockets, Scotty!" yelled Helen after the performance, leaping upon Jean from the bathroom doorway and tearing the other girl's dressing-gown pocket inside out. Eliza caught her eye and shook her head frantically. Someone might guess how suitable her role was if she kept this up.

Helen's high spirits infected the rest of them. They squashed together on the foot of her bed after Lights Out, recalling every detail of the play.

"You were *so* good, Helen," said Carrie. "You really were."

"Oh, it's just me natural self coming out. Did I look weird with my glasses on? I wouldn't have been able to see without them."

Carrie assured her she didn't and Eliza listened to their friendly talk with relief. Now that Carrie was certain of spending Easter with Eliza, she seemed much more willing to accept Helen as part of their threesome.

Helen tried to chin herself on the railing at the end of Eliza's bed. "It would be great to live on the streets like that, doing what you wanted. Which reminds me — we haven't had a dare for ages, not since Eliza's."

"I didn't think we were playing that anymore," said Carrie. They had all forgotten about the Daring Game. Eliza was surprised to discover she felt too old for it.

Helen rooted around in her blazer pockets for some paper. "This will be the last one, just to end the term. I haven't done one yet — neither has Scotty or P.J."

"You know I won't," yawned Pam, getting into bed. But even she was being more tolerant of Helen than usual. It was Helen's night.

Helen shook the hat and drew out a name. "It's Scotty! I was hoping it would be — I have a perfect dare for you."

"I don't think I want to play," Jean's voice wavered.

"You don't have to," said Pam. "Don't worry, Jean, they can't make you."

"But we'll all help you with it," entreated Helen. "Come on, Scotty, be a good sport. I heard something yesterday that gave me a great idea. You'll love it — you all will."

On the morning of the School Birthday the sun illum-
inated the whiteness of the freshly painted veranda
railing. Beside it an early cherry tree had unfurled its
delicate pink blossoms. Eliza noticed it on her way
into prayers. This leisurely Vancouver spring was
continually presenting her with new surprises. It was
so different from the prairies, where it was snow one
day, and mud and green leaves the next.

"Like the straightness of the pine trees/Le-et
me-e upri-ight be." She sang the words of the school
hymn with gusto, watching the very upright figure
of Miss Peck sitting in a wheelchair on the stage beside Miss Tavistock and the visiting Canon Finch. The
old woman sang resolutely, without a hymn book.
Then Miss Tavistock wheeled her aunt to the front
of the stage.

"My dear girls — I'm getting much too old for
long speeches, and I won't bore you with one this
year. But let me just congratulate you all on our
school's fifty-fifth birthday, and hope that we will
continue for fifty-five more years to uphold the
wise old traditions that have made Ashdown what it
is." They had to strain to hear her reedy voice. She
looked so slight in the wide, cushioned chair, as if
she had shrunk since Eliza had last seen her.

The Junior School presented homemade birthday
cards to Miss Peck and Miss Tavistock, and baskets
were passed for donations to the scholarship fund.

Then the prefects displayed their present to the
school — the new Canadian flag. Eliza admired it as
two of them held it up and everyone applauded. Its

crisp maple leaf flanked by bright red borders looked
so refreshing compared to the dingy Red Ensign
drooping beside the stage. Eliza was proud that
Canada now had its own flag. She remembered the
impassioned school debate about it a few months ago,
and a dinner-time conversation when she'd been at
Miss Tavistock's table. "I do think it's a shame to do
away with the symbol of the old country," the headmistress had begun. When the whole table drowned
her out with violent disagreement, she laughed and
said she supposed she'd better keep up with the times.

Now Canon Finch was speaking in his dry English voice. Eliza stopped listening and began to feel
apprehensive about what was going to happen during
lunch. It really was the best idea Helen had ever
had; and even if it didn't work, none of them could
get into trouble. But she wondered if Jean would go
through with it.

Eliza liked Jean and shared with her an addiction
to reading. Although Jean read nothing but animal
stories, she must have gone through every one that
had ever been written, and she had introduced Eliza
to a lot of new titles. Eliza sometimes recommended
books about other subjects, but Jean wouldn't touch
anything unless it had a dog or cat or horse in it.

Carrie only liked Nancy Drew mysteries, and
Pam and Helen never read outside school. Pam did
her required reading diligently and wrote neat book
reports that always got an A, but she often told Eliza
she should be out playing games instead of curled up
with a book. Helen couldn't understand why Eliza

and Jean would want to do anything that resembled school work for pleasure.

Jean was awfully quiet, however; she didn't let any of them get to know her very well. They all protected her, although Pam's protection was more like smothering. Certainly Jean had never before done anything as nervy as this dare.

The assembly sang the school song, then "Happy Birthday dear Ashdown." Eliza thought this was silly, but everyone was getting giddy anyhow, especially when the house captains burst through the door with an enormous cake, blazing with candles. There were a few informal classes before the day ended in a half-holiday. Eliza had hoped to say hello to Miss Peck, but she saw the white-haired figure leave in a taxi.

At lunch Eliza watched Jean speak to the prefect at the head of her table and slip out of the dining room. A few minutes later Helen left her chair, approached Ann, the head boarder, and whispered to her urgently. The older girl shook her head emphatically several times. Finally, however, Ann sighed, got up and said something to Miss Tavistock. The headmistress looked surprised. She glanced over at Helen, who was bent intently over her macaroni, and tapped the bell she always kept beside her at the table. "Your attention, please, girls. Helen Beauchamp has an announcement to make."

Helen skipped over to the dining room door and stood in front of its glass windows. "We have something to show you," she said simply, and opened the door.

Jean walked in with her arms full of a wriggling grey bundle. Behind her, her face flushing with embarrassment, was Jackie Chung, a day-girl from 7B.

"It's a dog! Oh, it's so cute! What's it doing *here*?" Pandemonium broke out, until it was quelled by the sharp *ting* of the bell.

"Girls, girls! Now Jean, what is all this about?"

Jean looked caught between laughing and crying. The small dog had crooked its front legs over her shoulders, as if it were hanging on. It trembled violently. "The-the Yellow Dorm would like to present this dog to the boarders as a birthday present," Jean squeaked, then put the dog on the floor and picked up the leash that trailed from its collar.

A universal "Ahhh . . ." filled the room, and chairs were scraped back as some people stood up to get a closer look.

Miss Tavistock stood up too, and banged the bell. Eliza watched her face; it looked stern, but she couldn't tell whether this was because of the noise or the dog.

"Sit down, everyone, and be quiet! You're frightening the poor animal. Now look, here is a surprise for your dessert." A tray of ice cream bars appeared from the kitchen, distracting some of the boarders' attention. "Everyone take one and go quickly outside — everyone except the Yellow Dorm. And Jacqueline, what are *you* doing here?"

Holly paused to stroke the dog on her way out. "Oh please, Miss Tavistock, can't we keep him?"

"We'll see, Holly, but I doubt it very much. Now hurry along outside. The rest of you sit down."

They sat in a row at one of the tables, and Eliza thought of the Yellow Dorm's feast, which seemed so long ago now. Jackie was at the end, the dog huddled on her lap.

Miss Tavistock half-smiled at them, but she looked bewildered. "Now, it is very nice of you to give the school a birthday present, but where did this dog come from? Is it yours, Jacqueline?"

Jackie nodded unhappily, but didn't seem to be able to speak. She buried her face in the wavy grey fur of the dog's neck.

"Pamela, you're the dorm head — suppose you explain."

"Oh, but Miss Tavistock, it wasn't *my* idea!"

Coward, thought Eliza. Pam had been just as excited about it as the rest of them.

Finally Helen explained, with help from Jackie, how the day-girl's family was looking for a new home for the dog "because we think my little brother's allergic to him."

"We thought he could live at the school. Then Jackie could still see him a lot, because she lives across the street. *Please*, Miss Tavistock," begged Jean, unusually bold.

"Who would take care of him?" The headmistress frowned, but patted the dog as he got down and sniffed her feet.

"*We* would," they chorused.

"What about the holidays? You can't expect the kitchen staff or the matrons to take on that responsibility, and I am certainly not going to. I really think,

Jacqueline," she continued gently, "that you'll have to find another home for him."

"I would take care of him in the holidays," said a gruff voice from the back. It was Mrs Renfrew, lurking at the other end of the dining room.

The Pouncer! Who would have thought *she* would help them out! The matron came over and picked up the dog. He stopped shivering and rested his head on her shoulders.

"The poor, wee thing," she murmured, in a purring voice none of them had ever heard before. "He is just like a dog I had as a child."

Miss Tavistock looked completely taken aback. "But Mrs Renfrew — surely you don't want the added work of an animal to look after!"

"I would like it very much. And Jean can help me," she added. Jean was the only boarder the Pouncer seemed to like, presumably because she had a Scottish background.

"Will you come into my study and discuss it? The rest of you wait out here and eat your ice cream. Jacqueline, you may have some too."

They gave the dog a whole bar to himself, broken up in a dish. He lapped it up daintily and Jean wiped the white drops off his whiskers.

"His name's Bill," said Jackie. "Oh, I hope it's all right. I could see him every day."

After a while Miss Tavistock came to the door and called in Jackie, saying she must phone her mother — that sounded hopeful. And ten minutes later it was decided: Bill would live at Ashdown, basing himself in Mrs Renfrew's room in the New Residence.

As the Pouncer and Jean led the dog away, and Jackie left reluctantly, Eliza wondered privately if the rest of them would ever be allowed near him. But just to have a dog in the school — even though he was such a small, timid dog and she preferred large ones — made it seem more like home.

"That *was* a wonderful dare," she told Helen, as the two of them and Carrie spent their half-holiday looking for lost tennis balls in the trees behind the courts.

"Mmmm . . . I told you so." Helen began to bounce a ball against the board fence. She looked more contented than she had all term; she also seemed to be getting thinner. When Carrie and Eliza started talking about what they would do in Seattle next week, Helen didn't seem to mind. It's because we're friends with her, Eliza realized. The only other friend Helen had was Linda O., but she and Helen mocked each other so much, Eliza wondered how close they really were.

"Uncle Adrian says he's going to take the three of us fishing at Campbell River in May," Eliza told them.

"Great! I'll show you how to catch a fish," said Helen. She stopped bouncing, and they sat in a row on the sun-warmed concrete, their backs against the fence.

"Are you coming back to Ashdown, Eliza?" said Carrie, breaking a companionable silence.

"Of course I am, silly! There's still one more

term." It amazed Eliza that, just a month ago, she wouldn't have wanted to come back. But now she was looking forward to it.

"I don't mean next term — I mean next year. Are you coming back for grade eight?"

"Aren't you?" said Helen, turning quickly to peer at Eliza. "I always thought you were!"

Eliza didn't know what to reply. First Beth had opened up the possibility of returning in grade ten — now these two were talking about next year. "I-I was always just coming for a year," she said, trying to avoid Helen's accusing stare. "I thought you knew that. I'll be going to school in Edmonton next year. An awful school — it's so big."

"Then why don't you come back?" demanded Helen.

"I don't know if my parents would let me. And anyway, I missed them a lot this term."

"So that's what was wrong with you!" said Carrie. "Well, I miss mine too, sometimes. Though I guess I see them more than you see yours." Helen said nothing, but threw the tennis ball away savagely.

Carrie nibbled the end of her braid. "Why don't you at least *ask* your parents if you could stay, Eliza? Then decide."

Eliza just wanted to change the subject. She was content with the present right now; she didn't want to think about the future. The cement under her was getting cold, even through her thick bloomers. She jumped up. "Oh, maybe I will. Come on, let's go and see Bill again."

Part III

Spring

XV

Bluebells

As Eliza and her aunt and uncle drove through the stone gates of Ashdown again, the first thing she noticed was a purply-blue haze that extended far into the woods. A mass of bluebells had sprung up in the two weeks she had been away. She remembered Miss Peck telling her that a bluebell was on Ashdown's crest because there were so many of them in Ashdown Forest. But she didn't know bluebells grew here as well. It seemed a good omen for the term ahead. Probably her last term. As soon as she realized that, she had a flash of herself, in future years, recalling the surprise of the bluebells. I'm missing it already, she thought. She said goodbye to her aunt and uncle impatiently, eager to get up to the dorm to see the others.

Eliza had spent half of her Easter holidays with Carrie, and half with Aunt Susan and Uncle Adrian. Seattle had been exciting. The United States was different from Canada. The people and places she saw seemed brighter and more defined; as if the U.S. was in colour, and Canada in black-and-white. Carrie's older brothers and sisters, home from college, had taken them on several excursions into the city. The rest of the time they had scurried in and out of the Olsens' large white house in Ballard, ridden bikes to Green Lake Park and helped out in the Scandinavian import store that Carrie's parents ran.

Everyone in the Olsen family had treated Eliza and Carrie like two amusing puppies whose every whim must be satisfied. The cook found out Eliza's favourite foods, and Carrie's grandmother lengthened one of her old dresses for her. It made a pleasant change to be the youngest in a family; no one expected anything of her.

Back in Vancouver, Eliza had a quiet week playing alone on the secret beach when the weather was dry and reading in the den when it was not. One day Aunt Susan took her down to The Bay to buy some new summer clothes. This turned into a battle. Eliza and her mother usually agreed about clothes. Aunt Susan, however, had an irritating preference for ruffles, extra flaps and zippers that had no function, and unnecessary accessories. "Wouldn't you like a purse?" suggested her aunt. "Here's a nice little white one. After all, you're almost a teenager — you'll want a bag to carry things in."

"I've got pockets," muttered Eliza, shaking her head. What a nuisance, carrying something extra around with you all the time! She refused barrettes for her straggling hair and insisted on getting it cut. Aunt Susan thought she should grow it out.

And her aunt wouldn't let her get everything in blue. "You need variety," she insisted, making her select a yellow and a pink T-shirt as well. Eliza's mother had always accepted her daughter's devotion to one colour. *She* understood that, if blue was your favourite, you wanted to wear it as much as possible. Eliza felt like saying it was her parents' money they were spending. But she always had to be polite to Aunt Susan because she did so much for Eliza.

While she was away from it, Eliza daydreamed a lot about returning to school, and she wondered what Helen was doing. She hoped she wasn't too miserable at home. The Chapmans had phoned at Easter and told Eliza they were all flying to Vancouver to pick her up in June. Only two months away; it seemed like no time at all. Now that she was going to see her parents so soon she forgot about missing them. She wanted this last term at Ashdown to pass slowly.

When Eliza assembled with the rest of the boarders that evening, she thought of bluebells again. Miss Tavistock had gathered them together to announce some sad news: Miss Peck had died during the holidays.

"She went in her sleep, very peacefully," said the headmistress, her face pale. She told them about the quiet family funeral and said that there would be a memorial service at the school next week.

After she dismissed them, several of the seniors stayed to express their sympathy. Eliza wanted to say something too, but she didn't know what. She hovered at the edge of the group and tried to absorb the fact that the spirited old woman, who had told her all about the Ashdown bluebell and had been interested in her on a particularly lonely day, no longer existed. In her mind, Miss Peck still sat erectly in her chair by the window in Crestwood Retirement Home.

Finally the last senior left. Eliza moved forward and murmured, "I'm sorry, Miss Tavistock. I liked Miss Peck."

"I know you did, Elizabeth." The headmistress put her hand on Eliza's shoulder. "She liked you too. She told me you were the kind of student she hoped Ashdown would produce."

As usual, Eliza was embarrassed to be labelled a model Ashdown student instead of just herself. But she was glad Miss Peck liked her. She went to bed filled with a kind of peaceful sadness.

The next morning before breakfast Miss Bixley measured them for their summer Sunday uniforms.

"It's *awful* — I can't wear it!" said Pam, throwing the white dress on the floor.

"Now don't be so fussy, Pam. Try this one."

"They look like nurses' uniforms," giggled Carrie. Eliza studied herself in the mirror and grimaced. The dresses were made of a slippery nylon material with permanently pleated skirts, sleeveless tops and peculiar short-sleeved jackets called "boleros" that went over them. Hers was more yellow than white and too big on top; it bagged over the narrow belt, but Miss Bixley said it was the closest fit she had. Ashdown students must have been wearing these for years. Eliza remembered an old photograph in the scrapbook Miss Peck had shown her, and the dresses had looked the same. She wondered how many students had worn hers.

At least the rest of the summer uniform was bought, not borrowed from the school. Eliza liked it even better than the winter one: a blue gingham cotton dress, white ankle socks and navy-and-white saddle shoes. It seemed a waste to wear it for only one term. Her shoes sparkled with newness, and she admired their gleam all the way down the stairs as she went out with Jean to take Bill for a walk.

Bill had turned out to be a very unsatisfactory kind of dog. He was frightened of most of the boarders and was always imploring Mrs Renfrew to pick him up. Jean was attempting to make friends with him again after her absence. After two days of constant attention he was fairly trusting of her, but he shrank from Eliza when she reached out to pat him.

They tried to make him fetch. He trotted obediently after the stick, but then just sat down and stared at it glumly. His bushy grey eyebrows made him look as if he were trying to work out some perplexing problem that was too much for him.

"What he likes best is to sleep on Mrs Renfrew's chair," said Jean. "I think he feels safe there." She crouched down. "Oh, poor little Bill, why are you so sad?" In answer the little dog stood up on his hind legs and hugged her neck. "He always does this," explained Jean, picking him up.

Eliza sighed, missing Jessie, who was bold and exuberant and loving to all. Only a few months until she saw *her*, too! But at least the addition of Bill to the school had changed Jean: she was much more purposeful, and sometimes she even stood up to Pam.

Pam had returned in a terrible mood. She seemed a lot older, somehow. She had a whole suitcase full of Beach Boys records and sophisticated outfits. And she looked as if she were wearing her new clothes even when she was in uniform. Her mother had flown from Geneva to spend the holidays in Vancouver with her daughter. But Pam had learned that her parents had to stay abroad another year, so she would be boarding again in the fall.

"Never mind," Carrie said when she'd told them this yesterday. "We'll all still be here. Except Eliza," she added in a different tone. Carrie had spent much of their time in Seattle trying to convince Eliza to ask her parents if she could return. Eliza had finally persuaded her not to talk about it, but the subject put a slight strain between them. And Eliza couldn't ask — she was too afraid her parents would say yes, and then she'd have to decide.

Pam wasn't consoled much by Carrie's remark. "I'd much rather be a day-girl again. Or I could go to school in Switzerland — think of all the skiing! But there's one good thing about staying in Vancouver. Norm will be here." She paused dramatically.

It was so obvious that she wanted them to question her further, that Eliza and Helen refused to. Carrie and Jean, however, took the bait: "Who's Norm?"

Norm was fourteen and a day-boy at St Martin's. He was the son of the family friends with whom Pam and her mother had been staying. "I've known him all my life, but I never really *saw* him before, if you know what I mean."

This was sickening; Eliza and Helen looked at each other with disgust. Eliza felt the same awkward embarrassment she had experienced in Seattle a few weeks ago when Carrie had taken her to a mixed party. Eliza had hidden in the kitchen, where she'd found the host's nine-year-old brother feasting on all the extra food. The two of them had a soothing game of Monopoly. Eliza had hated the way Carrie preened at the party, exactly the way Pam was acting now. But for the rest of the holidays her friend had been her usual everyday self. It was exasperating, as if Carrie were two different people, whereas Eliza always felt the same. The teenage silliness she'd hoped to avoid by coming to Ashdown seemed to be happening anyhow.

There was a miraculously long period of clear weather — not a drop of rain fell for two weeks. Spring was at its height, and the city was a fragrant garden. Eliza was enthralled by the variety of flowering trees she saw on their weekday walks through the neighbourhood streets. Each tree's blossoms blended with its new leaves to form a dappled canopy: white-and-green, white-and-copper, pale pink-and-copper, dark pink-and-green. The petals drifted in the air like snow and collected in heaps by the curb. Eliza and Carrie persuaded the matron to let them break away from the two-by-two crocodile line, scoop up the blossoms and throw them into the air like confetti.

To take advantage of the dry spell, there were lots of outdoor games: tennis and track-and-field, both of which Eliza loathed, and baseball, which she loved.

She almost always hit a home run. When she stood waiting for the ball to approach, she knew, somehow, when she was going to send it far off into the outfield with a satisfying wooden *crack*! Then she tore off madly around the bases. It was so exhilarating — everyone always cheered.

"You're a terrific asset when we're at bat," said Madeline. "But I wish you'd learn to catch and throw, Eliza." When they weren't up, Eliza was put into right field.

Madeline's mood this term was even more pensive, and Eliza had finally found out why. She was helping her house captain carry baseball mitts down to the playing field when a grade eleven day-girl passed them.

"I keep meaning to ask you, Madeline," she said, "did you have a good time in Kelowna? How was Brian?"

Madeline blushed. "We're in a hurry, Joyce," she mumbled. "I'll tell you later."

Eliza stared at Madeline. "Who's Brian?"

"Oh, just a boy I know. I met him at Christmas."

That explained a lot. But Madeline, too? Was sensible Madeline, who had once stated that she didn't agree with being "silly about boys," going to become as ridiculous about them as Pam?

"Don't look so shocked, Eliza," laughed Madeline. "I was going to tell you about Brian, but I wasn't sure you'd be interested. He's just a nice guy I like a lot. I miss him. Would you like to see his picture sometime?"

Eliza nodded reluctantly. First Carrie, then Pam and now Madeline — they were all going crackers. At least she and Helen were still sane.

Eliza sat happily at lunch one sunny Friday, waiting for a second piece of pie. There was an inter-house baseball game after school; Miss Clark had praised her essay comparing spring in Edmonton and Vancouver; and tonight they were all being taken to see *My Fair Lady*. Last but not least, she had been elected vice-president of 7A. The prospect had scared her, but she soon found out the job consisted of little more than waiting for each teacher in the hall before a class and walking behind her, carrying her books, to the classroom. There the president waited to shout, "Stand for Mme Courvoisier!" Having a position made her feel distinguished. So far, this term was a great improvement over the last.

"Save your tip," reminded Carrie beside her. You were supposed to cut off the tip of your piece of pie, eat it last and wish on it.

Miss Monaghan was taking the noon roll call to check on what each boarder was doing after school.

"Helen Beauchamp."

"Games, please, Miss Monaghan . . ."

"Elizabeth Chapman."

"Games, please, Miss Monaghan . . ."

"Pamela Jennings."

"Dorm, please, Miss Monaghan . . ."

"What's Pam up to?" whispered Eliza to Carrie. Staying in the residence after school was not encouraged, and Pam was such a tennis fanatic, she always said "games" instead of "walk."

"*I* know," said Helen, across from them. "I'll tell you later. Meet me in the gym before the game." Eliza swallowed her tip of pie and wished that Cedar would win.

They didn't. Oak, Helen and Carrie's house, won 10 to 7. Eliza had hit two home runs, but she'd missed five throws.

She and Helen and Carrie trudged slowly up the path from the playing field, stopping at the top to rest on a low bough of Eliza's tree. Eliza wiped her sweaty forehead and took deep sniffs of the tart smell of cut grass. She pulled off the sticky brown caps from the new tips of a fir tree.

Carrie squinted up at the Blue Sitting Room balcony across the lawn. "Are they there yet?"

"I don't see them," said Helen. "Let's just wait here. She can't spot us."

Helen had told them that Norm was visiting Pam after school. "He's bringing back a sweater she left at his parents' — I heard her asking Bix if it was all right for him to come. I bet that's just an excuse. They've probably got it all arranged."

Eliza pointed. "Look — there they are!" It was such a warm day, the door leading to the balcony was open. Through it they could see two standing figures.

The three of them scooted across the lawn and crawled into the thick laurel bushes under the balcony. Away from the sun it was chilly, especially with shorts on. Eliza shivered as she squatted and brushed the dirt from her knees.

"Shall we do it now?" whispered Carrie, trying to cover up her laughter with both hands.

"No! Wait and see if they come out onto the balcony." Helen frowned at her, and Carrie was still.

In a few minutes they heard footsteps overhead. At Helen's signal they moved over to the side so they could see the balcony more clearly.

Pam had changed into one of her new outfits, an orange-and-black striped dress and orange suède shoes. "She looks like a wasp," breathed Helen. The boy wore a maroon blazer, a yellow-and-maroon tie, which he was loosening, a crumpled white shirt and grey flannels. He had a round face and black hair that hung in his eyes.

Eliza stared at him curiously. He looked like any other boy. She didn't see what was so special about him.

"He's not so great," scoffed Carrie. "He has pimples!"

Pam was doing all the talking. "This is our recreation time. Normally I'd be playing tennis. Did I tell you I was in the Intermediate Finals?"

"Show-off," hissed Helen. "Okay, you guys — now!"

They opened their mouths and sang up as loudly as they could.

NORMAN! OOH-oo-ooh-oo-ooh-oo-
    ooh-oo-ooh
NORMAN! OOH-oo-ooh-oo-ooh-oo-
    ooh-oo-ooh
NORMAN! Norman my love!

His face turning crimson, the boy looked around wildly. Pam grabbed his arm and pushed him inside.

Eliza, Helen and Carrie tumbled out of the bushes and rolled around on the lawn in convulsions.

"Oh! Oh! I can't stop!"

"Did you see his face?"

"Did you see *hers*? It was perfect!"

"OOH-oo-ooh-oo-ooh-oo . . ." crooned Carrie.

Eliza clutched her stomach. "Stop!" she begged. "It hurts too much!"

"That'll teach her not to be so boy-crazy," pronounced Helen as they picked themselves up and hurried off to change.

Pam wouldn't speak to them for the rest of the day. That evening she had to go and see Miss Tavistock. On

Sunday Jean told them that the headmistress had been very upset about Norm's visit. "And Miss Bixley got told off, too," said Jean, her eyes round at the idea of her being the bearer of such gossip. "Boys aren't *ever* allowed to visit. Pam was supposed to wait and get her sweater yesterday."

Helen couldn't resist continuing the joke. "When's your boyfriend coming again, P.J.?" she said smoothly that evening. "We'd love to see him. You know, that was a good trick, the way you got him here. I think we could even count it as a dare."

Pam turned to face Helen, clenching her fists as if she were trying not to hit her. Then her face crumpled into tears. "I hate you, Helen! You're such a child, you and your stupid games. When are you going to grow up? *You've* never done a dare — you just give them to us. I bet you're afraid to."

Helen flinched, and her usually white face turned dull red. "You've never really done one either, have you, Pam?" she said softly. "I dare you to give *me* a dare. I'll do anything you like."

"What is all this commotion?" As usual the Pouncer appeared out of nowhere. "Get into bed at once. I'm turning out the lights and I don't want another word!" Unlike Miss Bixley, who would have tried to discover what the matter was, she didn't even notice Pam's tears.

After the matron left they waited to hear if Pam would answer. Eliza listened to her subsiding sobs and decided she would apologize to her tomorrow for their trick.

Finally Pam spoke, so quietly they could barely hear. "All right, Helen, I *will* give you a dare. And you'll be sorry, because it's much worse than anything you've ever thought of yourself."

XVI

A Tangled Web

The dare that Pam whispered to Helen that night was so risky that Eliza, Carrie and Jean all tried to talk her out of it the next morning. It would mean breaking one of the school's strictest rules.

"You'll get caught," said Carrie.

"And if you do, you'll be expelled," added Jean with a shudder.

These warnings just seemed to make Helen more determined. "Come on, Pam," pleaded Eliza, "say she doesn't have to do it. Or give her something easier."

"She doesn't have to do it," said Pam coolly, not looking at Helen. "It's up to her."

Helen glared at her. "I'll do it! I said I would, and I will. I'm not afraid. You'll all have to help me, though."

Eliza saw an escape route: surely Pam wouldn't take part, for then she might get into trouble too. But

Pam agreed; her anger made her unusually reckless.

Eliza considered that *she* could refuse to be involved, but that wouldn't stop them if Pam was going to help anyway. And if Helen insisted on doing this, she wanted to make sure she did it as safely as possible.

"We'll plan it tonight," said Helen. "At least there's still five more days until Saturday." For the first time, she sounded nervous.

Pam's challenge to Helen was to pretend to stay in on Saturday and then sneak out, stay away a few hours and return without being caught. They decided that Pam would come out with Eliza and Carrie to Eliza's aunt and uncle's, so Helen could meet them on the secret beach. "Otherwise," said Pam, "how would we know you'd done it? You could just say you had."

"Only you would do something like that, P.J.," retorted Helen. The two of them were more hostile than they'd ever been. It was as if the flames of irritation that had licked at both of them all year had flared up into a blaze of antagonism.

Eliza hoped her aunt would say she couldn't have any guests that Saturday, but Aunt Susan didn't mind. "Bring them both along," she said. "But what about Helen — doesn't she want to come too?"

"She — she has to stay in and catch up on some work," said Eliza. She hung up the phone feeling as if she had started events rolling and there was nothing she could do to stop them.

By the time Saturday morning arrived, however, they were beginning to feel excited about the dare. If

Helen succeeded, it would be the most thrilling thing they had done. And after all, thought Eliza, in her English boarding school books the girls often sneaked out, sometimes even at night. Compared to stories, just leaving the grounds for an hour or two seemed tame.

Now that Eliza had experienced a real boarding school, however, she was amazed at how easy it was for the jolly schoolgirls in her books to escape for midnight feasts on the cliffs, or forays into town. Even if they were caught, they had usually done something heroic, like catching a band of smugglers.

At Ashdown, she could too easily imagine Miss Tavistock's reaction to a student sneaking out on her own. And there was so much sharp-eyed supervision here that it was going to be very difficult for Helen to leave and come back without being detected.

They waited together in the hall to be picked up. Jean looked relieved to be going home as usual. They hadn't asked her to come because they knew she didn't want to take part.

Helen watched them leave, her round face particularly pale. "Goodbye, Helen!" Pam called back lightly as they trooped out the door with Uncle Adrian. "Have a good day!"

By one-thirty they were sitting on the beach, waiting for Helen to arrive. Carrie and Pam were collecting mussel shells. Eliza perched on the look-out, gazing at the sparkling blue sea. It was a perfect day. The water danced in lively little waves as if it knew something exciting was going to happen. Hundreds of white sails dotted English Bay. One boat close to them flapped wildly for a second, then caught the wind and glided by. The sun-heated driftwood gave off a tarry smell.

Eliza wondered how Helen would manage to escape. They had given her several suggestions, but so much depended on whether Miss Tavistock stayed in or went out. Luckily Matilda, not the Pouncer, was on duty for the day.

Already something had almost gone wrong. After lunch Aunt Susan had said, "Why don't we *all* go to the beach? The baby could play in the sand, and I'd like to tan my legs."

"Oh, but . . ." Eliza blushed, unable to continue.

"*I* know," teased her uncle, "you have some kind of private game going on, don't you?" Eliza nodded gratefully.

The other two joined her on the rock. It was quiet for a Saturday. Then a seagull screamed "*yow, yow*" from an adjoining rock, and a teenage couple appeared with a blaring radio. Eliza glanced at them coldly; she regarded the beach as her own property.

It was a quarter to two; where was Helen? She'd said she would leave the school at one. They watched the stone steps anxiously. "Maybe she won't come," said Pam. "I almost hope she doesn't — it *is* pretty dangerous."

Now you regret it, thought Eliza with exasperation. "She will," she said stiffly. "Helen's really brave."

Carrie turned her head, then jumped up. "There she is!" They waved frantically as a round red-headed figure in a green jacket approached from far down the beach.

Helen flopped down breathlessly. Her eyes shone as she tore off her jacket, fanned her dripping face and wiped her glasses. "Whew! I got off way past the stop, so I just came down to the beach and started walking back. I figured I'd see you eventually, as long as I headed this way. Got anything to drink?"

They pulled out the pop and sandwiches they had saved for her. Helen gulped half the bottle down in one swallow. Eliza watched her with admiration. Helen *was* brave. Even Pam had to admit it: "You did it, Helen," she said reluctantly, but her voice was fearful.

"Only half, though. I still have to get back." Helen grinned proudly. "It's great to think that no-body but you knows where I am."

There was almost an hour before she had to catch the bus back. They stretched out and roasted in the sun, and even paddled briefly in the icy water, while Helen told them how she had got away. "The rest of them went to a movie, but I told Matilda I was going to stay behind and study. She won't bring them back until at least four-thirty. After Charlie drove off, I just walked out the gate, then ran until I could wait for the bus without being seen. It was easy."

It wasn't easy to watch her leave. Helen didn't want to go so soon. "I could stay another hour," she complained. But the others, especially Pam, wanted her safely back at school.

"Do you have enough money?" she asked, as they walked to the bus stop.

Helen smirked wickedly at her. "Sure, P.J. Don't look so worried. This was *your* idea, remember."

They stood there apprehensively after the bus had carried Helen away, all the serenity of their hour in the sun spoiled. "This is the worst part," said Eliza, leading the others back to her uncle's house. "What if someone sees her come in?"

"They won't," said Carrie. "She has lots of time. Everyone will still be out except for the kitchen staff, and they won't notice."

"I still can't believe she actually did it," said Pam.

Afterwards, Eliza wondered what instinct made her say to her aunt, an hour later, "Can we go back to school now?"

"Now! But Eliza, what about dinner? I've just put the roast on!"

"I don't feel well," said Eliza. "I think my stomach is upset. I'm sorry, Aunt Susan, but I'd really rather go back now."

"Poor dear — but why don't you lie down here for a while?" Eliza insisted, however, and the others said they would return with her.

Eliza's stomach *was* upset, with anxiety, by the time they reached Ashdown. What if Helen wasn't there? And she hated the puzzled look on Aunt Susan's face. Eliza had always kept her boarding life and her

Saturday life in strictly separate compartments. This dare was mixing them up too uncomfortably.

There was no one in the hall to greet them. "Shall I go and look for a matron?" said Aunt Susan.

"It's all right," said Eliza hastily. "We'll find one."

They could hear the baby screaming in the car. "You be sure to tell her to put you right to bed, Eliza," said her aunt. "I'll phone you tomorrow to see how you are."

Miss Monaghan and nine boarders were in the dining room, noisily making lemonade. The matron looked up with surprise. "What are all of *you* doing here?"

"My aunt and uncle had to go out unexpectedly, so they brought us back early," said Eliza tightly. Another lie — how many had she told today? She thought of a Scott quotation they had memorized that week: "O what a tangled web we weave/When first we practice to deceive." But there were more urgent matters to worry about than lying: where was Helen?

Miss Monaghan squeezed a lemon vigorously. "That's too bad. But sit down and have some lemonade. Helen must still be studying over in the library — that's unusual! Why don't one of you go and fetch her? I have to lock the school building soon anyhow."

"I will!" offered Eliza.

She returned, puffing heavily, a few minutes later. "Helen says she doesn't want any lemonade. I don't either. Miss Monaghan, can we play outside un-

til supper? Carrie and Pam, do you want to come?"
She looked at the other two desperately.

Miss Monaghan shrugged. "As you wish. Supper
is at five — I'll ring the bell."

Helen had not returned. The three of them sat on the
swings in silence trying to absorb this fact. Struggling
not to cry, Eliza scraped the dust with her toe every
time her swing came forward.

They had searched everywhere — all the classrooms, the dorms, the gym, the tennis courts, the
woods and the playing field. "We'll just have to fake
it until she comes," said Eliza finally. "Maybe she's
only late."

"But she can't walk in the gate now. Someone
might see her!" said Carrie. Already Miss Tavistock's
little grey car had pulled up, and the matrons who
had the day off would return any moment.

Pam put on her dorm-head look. "I think we
should tell Miss Tavistock. Something could have
happened to her. Helen's not used to large cities. She
may have been hit by a car!"

"Or kidnapped!" added Carrie.

"Stop it!" Eliza stood up and faced them. She
couldn't check her tears now. "*Please,* let's wait a
little while at least. If we tell, we'll all be in terrible
trouble — especially Helen. She could still sneak in.
We just have to cover for her until she does."

Finally she persuaded them to wait two hours,
but Pam said she would tell after that. Eliza realized

there wasn't much choice — perhaps something *had* happened to Helen. But she pushed this thought out of her mind as they tackled the immediate problem of what to do about supper.

Sickness seemed to work as an excuse for anything. Now it was Helen who languished upstairs with an upset stomach. "I'll just nip up and check on her," said Miss Monaghan, turning into a nurse at once when they had told her this.

"Oh, no — she's gone to sleep and she doesn't want to be disturbed," said Carrie guilelessly. Eliza watched her earnest face; Carrie was a much better liar than herself.

"Well . . . after supper then," said Miss Monaghan. She showed them all how to make an Egg-in-a-Hole. Normally they would have enjoyed being allowed to cook, but none of the members of the Yellow Dorm could eat much.

After supper Eliza and Carrie dashed upstairs. Carrie got into Helen's bed and pulled the blankets over her face. Eliza drew the curtains and turned out the lights. Then they waited for Miss Monaghan.

"Is she any better?" the nurse whispered, peeking in at the door.

"Still asleep," said Eliza, coming out and closing it behind her. "I was just checking."

"She *should* go into the sickroom, but it probably isn't anything catching, and I don't want to disturb her. I have to go out now. You be sure to let

Miss Bixley know she's ill." Miss Monaghan hurried away humming. It was her night off, and she probably had someone to meet as usual.

They were fairly safe now until it was time to get ready for bed, and that was more than three hours away. Saturday evenings were usually a blur of confusion. People started returning from their days out around seven, and before that those who had stayed in could do as they liked.

Eliza, Carrie and Pam decided to watch TV. They had replaced Carrie under the covers with Pam's pink rabbit. With its ears folded back under its head, it looked just like a person rolled up in the blankets. Miss Bixley, who had returned and accepted their story easily, was now safely established in the matrons' sitting room.

Television made a convenient vacuum in which to think. Eliza stared at the screen blankly, her mind in a frantic whirl. Pam's two-hour grace period had passed, but she seemed to have forgotten, or else she was just working up her courage to tell.

What should they do? A horrible suspicion had lodged itself in Eliza's mind: what if Helen had run away? She remembered her look of contentment on the beach because nobody knew where she was. Eliza *thought* Helen seemed happier now, but it was always hard to tell with her unpredictable friend. Surely she would let Eliza know if she was planning something so drastic. But would she? Eliza remembered the Pound Money and wriggled with anxiety.

She had just decided they would have to go to Miss Tavistock, when the phone rang.

"It's for you, Eliza," called Miss Bixley. "It's your aunt."

Bother fussy Aunt Susan; Eliza hoped she hadn't told Miss Bixley she was supposed to be sick. Fortunately the phone was located in a private alcove away from all the sitting rooms and Miss Tavistock's study.

"Eliza? It's me. Don't act surprised, just listen very carefully. I had a hard enough time faking your aunt's voice."

Relief flooded through Eliza. "Are you okay, Helen?" she whispered.

"Sure, but I'm really in a fix. I did a dumb thing — I got off the bus and hung around Dunbar Street, and I forgot I had no more money to get on it again."

"Where *are* you?"

"In a park near the Dunbar Theatre. Have they discovered I'm gone?"

"Not yet. We're saying you're sick in bed."

"Great! Keep it up. I'll wait until it's dark and no one can see me, then I'll come up the fire escape."

"Oh, please be careful, Helen! We'll do our best." Eliza's hand trembled as she replaced the receiver.

She got Carrie and Pam away from the TV and they had another conference in the gym, after informing Miss Bixley they were going to practise basketball shots.

"We have to tell," insisted Pam, as soon as they

left the residence. "It's way past the time I said I'd wait."

"Shh!" Eliza hurried her inside the gym door, then she told them. "Helen phoned! She's okay! It could all work out now, Pam, you have to see that! She's counting on us."

Carrie was worried about Helen wandering the streets on her own. Pam was even more reluctant. "Something could still happen to her, especially when it gets dark. It's just not right not to tell someone." But Eliza finally convinced them that, if Helen could get in safely, all of them would escape Miss Tavistock's wrath and the risk would be worth it.

Jean arrived back at eight. Their story terrified her so much that they knew she wouldn't say anything. The rabbit-dummy of Helen dozed on peacefully. When Miss Bixley appeared at a quarter past nine, their lights were already out. "In bed so soon? Good girls. Now no chattering, so you don't wake Helen. Goodnight, everyone."

Lying in the darkness, Eliza felt some of the extraordinary tension of the day disappear. All they could do now was wait. At least she could stop worrying about concealing Helen's absence; now she just had Helen herself to be anxious about. She tried to fill in the gaps in the brief account Helen had given on the phone. What had she been doing all this time? And where was she now? She was taking so long . . .

Pam got out of bed. "Where are you going?" Eliza asked her jumpily.

"Just to the bathroom — don't be so suspicious, Eliza."

Suspicious? Why would she be suspicious? She didn't have time to think of a reason, because as soon as Pam had disappeared there was a tap at the window, and in tumbled Helen.

"Let go, let go!" she gasped, as Eliza hung around her neck, and the others all started talking at the same time. "Just let me get undressed and then we'll be safe."

She scrambled into her pyjamas and jumped into bed, pitching out the rabbit with a chuckle. "Whew! What an incredible day! I'll never do *that* again! Wait till you hear . . ."

Eliza could only half-listen, she suddenly felt so drained. Some things were too exciting. But everything was all right now.

Then Helen stopped in the middle of a sentence. "Where's Pam?"

Before they had time to wonder, there were sharp rapid footsteps in the hall; then the lights flooded the room. "So you're back, Helen. Get up, everyone," said Miss Tavistock, in the coldest voice Eliza had ever heard her use, "and tell me if what Pamela has just told me is true."

XVII

Isolation

There were no tears left to cry. Eliza lay on the narrow sickroom bed and stared at the darkening sky outside the window. It was the same bed she'd been in when she was here in March. Part of her thought fleetingly of how much she had already cried into this mattress. But that period in the sickroom had turned into a healing rest; this time was becoming worse and worse.

She was in solitary confinement. Somewhere over in the New Residence, Helen, too, was isolated in a room. Or perhaps she had already left. How did they expel someone? Would she be smuggled away at dawn? Would Eliza ever see her again?

Her ears rang with words, all the words that had crowded the air in Miss Tavistock's study, spoken last night and today. She tried to stop them, but they kept repeating themselves in a relentless chorus. And the dominating voice was Miss Tavistock's.

First they had all been interviewed together, huddled on the couch, while the clock outside the study chimed the late hour. Eliza was squished between Helen and Carrie, their bodies pressing against hers with a comforting warmth.

The story had emerged quickly, drawn out by the headmistress's piercing questions. It became painfully evident how large a part Eliza had played, by agreeing to stage the dare at her aunt and uncle's in the first place and by being the ringleader of the concealment. Eliza was glad that Pam's initial role was also revealed; but she knew that, by telling, Pam had cancelled out much of her wrongdoing. At least nothing had been said about any of the other dares. Miss Tavistock still thought this was a single occurrence.

"I am not going to tell you tonight," she said, in the same icy voice she'd used all during the interview, "what I think of this dreadful behaviour, except to say you are in very serious trouble. Helen and Elizabeth, you will each sleep in isolation. The rest of you go upstairs without a word. None of you will go to church, and I will speak to each of you separately tomorrow."

Eliza woke up with the Sunday rising bell and was handed a breakfast tray and her clothes by a silent and disapproving Mrs Renfrew. She choked down some bacon and toast, terrified of the approaching interview. It was so lonely, not being able to talk to the others — at least Carrie, Jean and Pam had that consolation. Ever since the lights had flashed on last night, she had felt as if she were dreaming.

It wasn't until the end of the morning that she was finally back in the headmistress's study. At least she was being allowed to sit down. Miss Tavistock, erect in her straight-backed chair, looked tired. Her usually immaculate hair was escaping in wisps from its bun. Eliza glanced once into her clear blue eyes, then looked away. She also avoided the eye of Miss Peck, looking down at her reproachfully from the portrait. I will *not* cry, she thought stubbornly and dug her thumbnail hard into her little finger to keep from doing so.

The first sentence of the lecture was the hardest to bear: "I am talking to you last, Elizabeth, because it is you in whom I am most disappointed." Then the headmistress proceeded to list all of Eliza's transgressions.

Eliza felt removed; she could only whisper, "Yes, Miss Tavistock," at appropriate intervals. Shocked at her detachment, she noticed that everything Miss Tavistock was saying began with a "D": "Deceit," "Deliberate Defiance," "Dangerous," and "Disloyalty." As the level voice continued she squirmed with guilt, wishing the headmistress would finish telling her what she already knew and get on to the most important part: What was going to happen to her? And to Helen?

When the stinging words finally ended, Eliza tried to make her voice work without her ready tears interfering. "I'm sorry, Miss Tavistock. It was a stupid thing to do, although we didn't know it would turn out to be so complicated, and we didn't deliberately rebel against the school. I really am sorry." She sat limply and waited for the headmistress to pronounce her sentence.

Miss Tavistock's large eyes looked at her for a few seconds, and Eliza's tears finally overflowed. The headmistress's voice became less stern as she handed over her handkerchief. "All right, Elizabeth. I think you know all the wrong things you've done, and I'm not going to tell you any more of them. I haven't yet decided what your punishment will be. But now I want to talk to you very seriously about Helen."

Eliza checked her crying and listened rigidly. The tears dried around her eyes, cooling them.

"When I first noticed the friendship between you and Helen I was pleased, although surprised, to see it. I thought you would be a good influence on her, and that appeared true — she seemed to be improving greatly this year. But it was a false hope. This incident proves to me that Helen has been a bad influence all along, on you and on the others."

She stilled Eliza's objection. "No, listen to me, Elizabeth. Helen is obviously the instigator of this prank. Yes, I know it was Pamela's idea, but Helen herself has said she provoked Pamela into it. She admits it was all her fault — and was very adamant, by the way, that it wasn't yours."

"But we *all* did it, Miss Tavistock! Helen wouldn't have tried it alone. We chose to help her. She didn't influence us." Eliza was beginning to feel angry and puzzled. She knew how high up on the Ashdown scale of offences their crime was, but surely it didn't warrant *this* much fuss.

"If it were an isolated incident I would agree with you, Elizabeth. But Helen has fooled us all.

There is a difference between behaviour which is un-thinking foolishness, like yours, and that which is sly and deliberate. I used to think Helen was simply too full of high spirits for her own good. I now have reason to believe she is more devious than she appears — that she is, in fact, a thief."

Every nerve in Eliza's body became taut. She felt she was going to snap. The inside of her mouth dried up, and she tried desperately not to let the headmistress see she was reacting in any way to this statement.

Miss Tavistock continued. "Has Helen ever told you that she was sent to Ashdown because she was accused of stealing?" Eliza nodded warily. "I don't make a policy of taking problem children here — that's not what the school is for. But Helen's grandmother is an alumna, and when she wrote to me about Helen I could see that there were other difficulties at home as well. Helen was very young and unhappy at the time, and I'm not certain she knew what she was doing."

"She didn't do it!" exclaimed Eliza. "She was just hanging around with those kids!"

"She once told me that herself, and I was almost convinced. But now I am not so sure." Miss Tavistock sounded perplexed. "You see, Elizabeth, Mrs Crump, from across the street, phoned me this morning. She says Helen stole some licorice from her store last evening. That would have been while she was waiting to come in. Helen denies it, but not very strongly. I simply don't know what to think, because there's the episode about the Pound Money last term, which Helen also denies, as she did in January. I have no proof that she was the culprit in that case, and I don't wish to be unfair. But now that she's been accused of stealing for a second time, I can't help suspecting that she may have stolen before. Now, I want to ask you a very important question, Elizabeth."

Eliza's mind raced frantically. She pressed her shaking knees together and waited.

"You know Helen better than any of us. Have you ever seen evidence of her stealing while she's been here? Now, don't answer for a minute. Just listen carefully and think about what I'm saying."

Miss Tavistock sat up straighter. "It was very wrong of you to cover up for Helen yesterday. I know you did it out of loyalty to her, and I do admire loyalty, but you must also be loyal to the school. I simply cannot have an underhanded, dishonest girl living in a close community that depends on trust among its members. I'm sure you see that. You have demonstrated to me ever since you've come here that you understand Ashdown's principles. Now, which is more important — the welfare of all the students, or of just Helen?"

A myriad thoughts filled Eliza's mind. The few seconds she took before she replied seemed an eternity.

She had never really been sure of Helen. The other girl could have been lying to her all along, and Miss Tavistock's revelation bewildered her so much that part of her longed to pour out her confusion to the headmistress.

But Helen was her friend. That was a solid, unalterable fact. She looked at Miss Tavistock and saw a friend also. A fair and kind woman who collected stamps and let the boarders have a dog. She also saw a person who was very clear about what was right and what was wrong. Just as clear as Eliza suddenly was.

Miss Tavistock was watching her steadily. Eliza could sense her thoughts, as she often could with adults: "It is a lot to ask of her, but I trust her to come through." For an instant they were not an adult and child, but two equals.

Then Eliza answered. "Helen would *never* steal, Miss Tavistock — she's honest! I even asked her about the Pound Money once, because of what she told me about coming here. She was really upset I'd suspect her, and she'd never lie to me — I'm her best friend." She tried to make her eyes wide and innocent, the way Carrie had when she'd lied to Miss Monaghan. "Mrs Crump doesn't like Helen. She doesn't like any of us. I'm sure she made a mistake."

"Thank you, Elizabeth," said the headmistress quietly. "I respect your honesty."

There was a long silence. Eliza studied Miss Tavistock's stapler. She had never noticed before exactly how a stapler was constructed. She had also never felt so alone in her life.

Then came the worst part of all. Miss Tavistock sighed and said, "I would like to believe Helen as you do, Elizabeth. But I'm afraid she has fooled you also. The evidence is all against her, and I'm going to have to remove her from the school."

Eliza leaped to her feet. "No! You can't do that, Miss Tavistock!"

"Please sit down, Elizabeth, and control yourself. I have no choice. A student who steals and then
lies about it is simply too bad an influence. I know
this is very painful for you," she added gently, "because she is your friend. But that is my decision."

For a few seconds Eliza sat frozen with disbelief.
Helen expelled! Then anger swelled in her and she
stood up again. "You *can't* make Helen leave! This is
all she has! She likes it here," she continued, suddenly
realizing that it was true. "She likes it more than any
of us, more than I do!" She heard herself beginning to
shout. "It's so unfair! Helen is only twelve, and you're
ruining her life, and you're *wrong*, you're *wrong* . . ."
Now all she could do was choke back her sobs.

Miss Tavistock stood up too. "Elizabeth, you
must not speak to me this way!" Eliza looked at her
fuzzily. In the blue eyes she saw a mixture of anger,
hurt and sympathy. Miss Tavistock took her by the
shoulders and steered her to the door. "You'd better
return to the sickroom. You can remain there until
you're ready to apologize."

Eliza fled. She slammed the sickroom door,
threw herself down on a bed and wept bitterly until
she could cry no more.

Now she wondered indifferently if she would have to
live in the sickroom for the rest of the term, for she
would never apologize. It didn't matter if she stayed
here — all that mattered was Helen.

Even if she never came back to Ashdown herself,
she couldn't imagine Helen not being here. It was un-

thinkable. Expulsion was something she'd always heard of but never expected would actually happen to anyone she knew.

She tossed restlessly, wondering if Helen *had* stolen again. Red licorice was her friend's passion, and she must have been hungry by the time she had come back to the school.

Was she right to lie so much to defend Helen? Even if she was, it hadn't done any good. In a book it would have. Miss Tavistock would have been so convinced by Eliza's loyalty that Helen would have been saved.

She suddenly felt young and weary, too young for all the things everyone expected of her. People like her parents and Miss Tavistock expected her to be truthful. Helen expected her to be loyal. She drew a blanket over her head, curled up into a ball and wished she could run away from all of them, the way she had once in her dream.

Outside the door, a soft melody came from the Blue Sitting Room piano: three notes rising up, then repeated. It sounded so familiar . . . the *Moonlight* Sonata.

Creeping to the door, she peeked in. Madeline was sitting at the piano in the corner of the shadowy room. The music stopped, and the dark-haired girl turned to look at her. "I thought that would bring you out. I was going to knock if it didn't. Come and talk — no one will see us. They're all singing in the dining room."

Eliza hadn't heard them, but now she did. Someone was playing a guitar, and the mournful strains of a folk song floated down the hall: "Sometimes I feel like a motherless child/Long way from ho-ome . . ." It made her want to cry again. She looked hopelessly at the older girl.

Madeline patted the couch. "Sit down over here, Eliza. You don't have to tell me anything if you don't want to. I just wanted to know if I could help."

"P-please — do you know if Helen's still here?" Eliza finally stammered.

"She must be — I just saw a tray go into the room she's in. What on earth is going on? You should hear the rumours! Can you tell me?"

Eliza tried. She didn't say anything about the earlier stealing episodes, however, or about her lie. Madeline listened to the convoluted story thoughtfully. She was so calm that Eliza felt a tiny bit better.

"It *was* a crazy risk to take," she said at the end. "But you know that. Poor Helen. I'm sure she didn't steal anything. It's not like Charlie, to go as far as expelling her. I'd believe Helen over Crabby Crump any day."

Eliza was glad she couldn't tell Madeline about all the other evidence besides Mrs Crump's. "She *said* she would expel her. I got really mad at her. I'm supposed to apologize, but I won't. And I did something else, too, which I can't tell you. It was *right* — but nobody else would think so, maybe not even you."

"Nobody's responsible for your decisions but yourself, Eliza. If you think it was right, then you have to accept it."

"I guess so," agreed Eliza sadly.

"You know, you may as well apologize. Why prolong all of this? Helen's the most important person we have to worry about right now."

"Oh, Madeline — nothing will ever be the same! I can't imagine the rest of this term without Helen."

"Neither can I. She livened everything up. She was a nuisance, but I liked her."

Eliza couldn't bear this — they were talking about Helen as if she were dead. She stood up to go, but Madeline stopped her. "I'm sorry, Eliza. It's terrible, but I can't think of anything we can do. If I can, I'll let you know. Maybe Miss Tavistock will change her mind."

But Eliza knew the headmistress had meant what she said. She appreciated Madeline's concern, but there really was no way she could help. She felt older, not younger, than the other girl.

Madeline seemed to sense this also. She looked ruefully at Eliza. "Do you remember that talk we had a long time ago, about growing up?"

Eliza nodded miserably.

"Well," said Madeline, "I think you've begun."

Eliza spent the next few hours working up the courage to sneak out of the sickroom and try to see Helen. She decided to do it after someone had come to tell her to go to bed, but no one did. The house settled into silence. She had just put on her pyjamas when she was called back into Miss Tavistock's study.

"I'm sorry I was rude," Eliza mumbled as soon as she sat down. She wanted to say it before Miss Tavistock asked her to.

"I accept your apology, Elizabeth." The headmistress sounded sorry herself. Her voice was fairly cheerful, and Eliza watched her suspiciously. Now what was happening? If she thought they could be friends again, she was wrong.

"What you and Helen and the others did yesterday was very serious," Miss Tavistock began. "But I'm happy to be able to tell you that the other charge against Helen has been dropped."

All of Eliza's indifference flew away in a rush. She clenched her fists and waited.

"Jacqueline Chung was here this afternoon, visiting her dog. I overheard her and Linda O'Hara discussing Helen's prank, although how they heard about it I don't know. Jacqueline told Linda she had seen Helen at the store yesterday. So I questioned her — *she* had given Helen the licorice. When Mrs Crump saw her after closing the store she assumed Helen had taken it, since she'd been lingering in there all evening. I have phoned and told her that Helen did not steal anything."

"Oh, Miss Tavistock," breathed Eliza with shining eyes. "Does that mean she won't be expelled?"

"I wasn't going to expel her this late in the year, although I *was* going to ask her not to return. But yes, now she can stay. It is obvious she isn't a thief, and I apologize to you, as I will to Helen, for suspecting that she took the Pound Money. Perhaps you will return next year also, Elizabeth — although I must say I've had enough of both of you at the moment."

This was almost a joke, and Eliza grinned. She was so happy she wanted to laugh, but then Miss Tavistock became stern again. "Now let's talk about the other matter. Helen is to be grounded for a month, and you are for three weeks. That means no walks, no films, no Saturdays out and no Victoria Day weekend — you are not to leave the school property. Pamela and Caroline are being grounded also, for a lesser time, and Pamela is no longer your dorm head. You have not shown me that any of you are responsible enough for that position, and Miss Bixley will just have to supervise you more closely. Each of the four of you will apologize to the matrons who were on duty that day, as well as to your aunt and uncle."

Eliza barely listened to these penalties. None of them mattered, as long as Helen was saved.

"You may go back up to your dormitory now, but I don't want you to discuss this endlessly, do you understand?"

Eliza nodded and shook the headmistress's hand fervently. "*Thank* you, Miss Tavistock! We'll be so good, you won't believe it!"

"I'm sure I won't," said Miss Tavistock dryly. "Go on to bed, Elizabeth. It's late, and I still have Helen to speak to."

Carrie, Jean and Pam were crowded together on Carrie's bed when Eliza threw herself into their midst. Carrie clutched her so hard that Eliza yelped in protest. "Oh, Eliza," the other girl whispered. "I missed you! I was so relieved when Miss Tavistock told us you and Helen weren't expelled. We really thought you might be. But where is she?"

"Talking to Miss Tavistock." Eliza released herself from Carrie's grasp and punched a beaming Jean on the arm. Then she looked at Pam. She didn't know what to say to her.

"I'm sorry, Eliza," said Pam quickly. "I couldn't help it. I *had* to tell. Helen was taking so long."

Part of Eliza knew she'd never forgive her. She also knew that Pam would never change. Pam, like herself, had only done what she'd thought was right.

"At least it wasn't worse," Eliza said finally. "At least we're all still together." They sat quietly in the dark and waited for Helen.

XVIII

What Really Happened

Because Miss Tavistock had warned them not to, the others were afraid to talk much about what they came to refer to as "the last dare." But Eliza had to know exactly what had happened, and after school on Monday she dragged Helen off to the edge of the woods to hear the whole story.

They leaned against two tree trunks. It was forbidden to go right into the woods, and although they often did, neither had the energy to break a rule today. Eliza's nerves were still so jangled that it was a relief to collapse on the cool grass. Helen looked just as frazzled — pale, tired and unusually quiet.

"Okay . . . why did you get off the bus?" Eliza prompted.

Helen sounded incredulous, as if she were talking about someone else. "Well, it was still early. It seemed a waste to go back so soon. I figured I could hang around Dunbar for at least an hour."

"But you haven't got a watch!"

"Don't I know it! I should have borrowed yours. I just kept asking people the time. I wandered around all the stores." She sounded wistful. "That part was great, being able to go wherever I wanted. Then the ticket man at the movie asked me if I wanted to go in for the last part — he said it wouldn't cost me anything. And he *said* there was only half an hour left. But when I came out the theatre clock said four-fifteen!"

"But didn't you realize it was longer when you were watching it?"

"I got too interested. It was James Bond, and it was terrific! I was going to go back then anyhow, even though it would be risky. I would've just made it by suppertime. But then I realized I didn't have bus fare! So I phoned your aunt's — I thought you guys would think of something."

"How did you, without any money?"

"First I looked up the number in the phone booth — that took forever, there are so many Chapmans. Then they let me use the phone in the library. And your aunt said you'd gone back to school. Why did you, by the way?"

"I don't know," said Eliza. "I just sort of felt something was wrong."

"Well, I was glad in one way because I knew you'd bluff for me somehow."

"It didn't do any good in the end, though."

"It might have. Thanks for trying, anyhow. It must have been tricky."

"It *was,*" said Eliza. "I never want to have to go through that again! But what did you do then? You could have walked, I suppose."

"That's what I decided to do, but it was already too late. I couldn't just stroll into school after supper — what would I say? Especially when I didn't know what kind of story you'd cooked up about me. I wanted to phone the school to find out, but they made me leave the library when it closed. So all I could think of was not coming back until everyone was in bed."

"What did you do all that time?"

"I stayed in the park there for a while. There was a baseball game going on. That's where I found a dime in the phone booth and called you. Then I walked back and hung around in Crabby Crump's, reading magazines. She couldn't stand that, of course, so she finally kicked me out. Then she . . ." Helen's voice became low and angry, and she stopped.

"I know what happened then," Eliza said quietly. "Miss Tavistock told me. Crabby Crump accused you of stealing."

Helen kicked the grass. "I couldn't believe it, after everything else that day! There I was, sitting innocently on the bench outside the store, waiting for the sun to go down. And Jackie and her older sister came by. They talked to me for a while, and I told them I'd sneaked out to go to the store. They laughed — they think we do stuff like that all the time! Luckily

Jackie's sister doesn't go to Ashdown. *She* didn't care, in fact she thought it was great. Anyhow, they went in and bought some red licorice, and gave me some. Did I ever need that! And later Crump closed the store, saw me eating it outside and accused me of stealing it."

"What did you say?"

"I told her the truth, but she didn't believe me, of course. She walked away muttering to herself, the way she always does. I forgot all about it until Charlie said she'd phoned. And then Charlie didn't believe me."

"But why didn't you tell her about Jackie?" This was what Eliza found the hardest to understand.

Helen's eyes receded behind her glasses, as if she couldn't remember. "I don't know . . . Once she mentioned stealing, I just sort of clammed up, it seemed so useless to defend myself. Especially when . . ." She paused.

Eliza said nothing; they were both thinking about the same thing.

"Do you know," Helen continued slowly, "I almost *told* her about the Pound Money? Not the first time she asked — I-I didn't feel like saying anything more then — but when she apologized later. It didn't seem right to let her think I wasn't a thief when I was. I probably should have told her . . ."

Eliza hated the shame in her friend's voice. This wasn't Helen! Helen was strong and daring, not downcast like this.

When she thought about it, though, it occurred to her that, deep down, Helen was always afraid. That explained why she was so brash all the time: she had to be, to cover up her fear. It was embarrassing to know this — and to know that Helen knew she knew. It made a bond between them they could never talk about.

"I'm glad you didn't tell her," Eliza said quickly. "You didn't *want* to have to leave Ashdown, did you?"

"I guess not," Helen admitted. "I'm not old enough to be on my own, so I may as well be here. I sure don't want to live at home."

"I thought you might have run away," murmured Eliza.

Helen looked at her with amazement. "You did? Where would I go? Maybe once I would have considered it — before this year. But things are better here now. Or else I've changed." Helen hesitated, then continued slowly. "Eliza . . . did you think I had stolen something again? I wouldn't have, you know, no matter how hungry I was. I guess I just don't need to anymore."

Eliza thought she might as well be truthful. "I did wonder," she confessed, "but I hoped you hadn't." There seemed no point in telling Helen she had lied for her. "And of course, you didn't," she said warmly. "You *have* changed."

Helen absorbed this in silence, as if she weren't quite sure that it was true.

"Tell me the rest!" urged Eliza. "Was it scary to sneak in?"

"That part was the easiest. I came in the back gate and ran across the grass to the fire escape. Lucky all the curtains were pulled in the matrons' sitting room. Not that it made any difference," she added gloomily. They both sat and pondered how near she had come to being safe.

"I can't believe so much happened in just two days," said Eliza finally.

"Neither can I," said Helen. "In fact, I would even be glad if nothing else happened for a while."

XIX

"Those Returning"

It was the morning of Graduation Day, and all of the boarders except the graduates were putting out the chairs for the second time. Right after breakfast they had taken them from the gym and placed them in careful rows on the lawn. Then the sky darkened and a few drops of rain fell: back to the gym went the chairs, to be set up in there. But just before lunch it cleared up again, and Miss Tavistock decided to take a chance on the weather. "So much nicer to have the ceremony outside," she said.

"Why can't she make up her mind?" grumbled Helen, unsuccessfully trying to carry three chairs at once. "You'd think we were slave labour."

Eliza rescued a falling chair and added it to hers. Helen was certainly her old self again, after being subdued for a long time. During the weeks of their mutual confinement to the grounds, the Yellow Dorm had stuck close together — especially Eliza and Helen, whose sentences had been the longest. Now they were all free. Two weeks ago Eliza had finally been able to go out on Saturday, and last week Helen had come too. Uncle Adrian had taken them fishing. Helen was the only one who caught a salmon.

"It's hard to believe the year is almost over," said Eliza. They stopped to rest, hiding behind a bush so they wouldn't be caught. "Only one more week!"

"Don't keep saying that!" complained Helen. "Then you're leaving for good."

Eliza looked at her sadly. The hardest person to leave behind was Helen. Harder than Carrie, who had promised to come to Edmonton in August. Eliza knew Helen's parents would never send her on a visit.

A letter from Eliza's mother had decided her future:

> . . . Dad and I have been wondering if you're going to want to return to Ashdown next year, since you've enjoyed it so much. But I'm afraid we just can't manage it right now after all the extra expenses of this year. Besides, we do think you're still a bit young to be away from home, especially when there's no longer a reason for it. We'll see about sending you back in grade ten, if you want to go then.
>
> I hear from Susan you've been up to some mischief! You're certainly going to miss all the fun you've had and the friends you've made . . .

Eliza reacted to the last sentence first. "Fun" and "mischief" indeed! Aunt Susan and Uncle Adrian were the same — they'd been eager to hear the whole story of the dare. "You girls are little devils," Uncle Adrian had chuckled after Eliza had reluctantly told them a censored version. Her family would never understand how serious it had been.

Then the import of the letter sank in. She wasn't coming back. With distaste, she reflected on the ugly modern school she would have to attend in Edmonton, all the dreaded activities that went on in that building, and the old friends from whom she now felt so distant.

After this year, however, she felt braver. Perhaps she could look upon Westview Junior High School as a kind of dare.

And she pictured being free from that school every day at three o'clock, riding her bike home and doing what she liked: reading in her own room that she'd organized to perfection, exploring the river valley with Jessie, playing cribbage with her father before dinner.

The world within Ashdown's stone walls was secure and full of beauty — but lonely, too. The other world was disagreeable and uncomfortable, but it was where her family and home were. She couldn't have decided between the two, and most of her feelings after reading her mother's letter had been relief at not having to.

The worst part was leaving Helen. "I'll see you *sometime*," she assured her now. "We'll be back in Vancouver to visit. If it's not during the holidays we'll come and sign you out. Won't that be weird? I'll be an outsider then . . ."

"Oh, I'll survive," said Helen blithely. "I'll find another new girl to train. Lots of kids come in grade eight."

Eliza flinched; it was still so easy to be hurt by Helen. Then she reminded herself that nonchalance was her friend's usual way of covering up her real feelings.

"Did I tell you," Helen continued casually, "that I'm going to be in the upper grade eight class next year?" Helen's marks had improved simply because she'd spent so much time studying in the past weeks. There'd been almost nothing else to do during their confinement.

"Do you want to be?"

"I guess so. It doesn't mean I'm turning into a brain like you, Eliza Doolittle," she added hastily, "but it's a change. And Charlie's going to ask my parents if I can take acting lessons on Saturdays."

"Will they let you?"

"Sure . . . they'll just get my grandmother to pay for it."

"I'll write to you all the time, Helen," promised Eliza. "And you have to write back and tell me everything that's happening."

"I will — you'll be shocked!" Helen looked down at the rose petal she was shredding. "And some day we'll both be finished school. Maybe we can travel together or something . . ."

That was a relief. Eliza's deepest worry was that the other girl would forget about her.

"Do you *want* to get older?" she asked Helen curiously as they picked up their chairs again.

"Of course. I want to grow up and be free! To be finished with school *and* my family and just be on my own."

"But it's awful, all the things you have to go through as a teenager."

"Sure it is, but you have to go through them to get any older, don't you? And I don't intend to ever get as goony as Pam. Nobody's going to make me do anything I don't want to."

Eliza studied her friend for a few seconds and decided that probably nobody ever would.

After lunch she balanced on the railing and listened to Madeline practise "Land of Hope and Glory" on the piano that had been moved onto the balcony of the Blue Sitting Room. Eliza was all ready for the ceremony, dressed in her clammy white dress. She rubbed her shiny legs against each other, making them scratch; the grade sevens were being allowed to wear nylons for the first time. Below them the chairs were finally settled in long empty rows that would be filled in an hour with students and parents. Jean was racing a reluctant Bill, on his leash, around and around the lawn. The others were still upstairs changing.

The last swelling notes of the march ended. It was so solemn, it made Eliza shiver. Madeline would play it for the opening procession. "You're going to get your dress dirty, sitting there," she told Eliza.

Madeline was not coming back next year either. Mrs Fraser said she could take her no further in piano, and so Madeline was going to live with relatives in Toronto and attend the Royal Conservatory of Music. Eliza felt better about leaving herself when she knew Madeline was going too.

"It's funny," mused Madeline. "On graduation days I always used to imagine how it would feel, to march up the middle to this music. Now I never will."

"What about Brian?" asked Eliza. It was the first time she had mentioned him since the beginning of the term. "When Beth told me you had plans for next year, I thought maybe you were going to go to school in Kelowna so you could be near him."

"I wouldn't do that! What about my piano lessons? No, I've known Toronto was in the works for a long time — it just took a while to get it organized. I'll miss Brian a lot, but we have plenty of time. My music is the most important thing to me now."

Eliza grinned. "Maybe you'll be famous one day and I can say I knew you." She paused. "Madeline . . . can I write to you sometimes?" It had taken days to work up the courage to suggest this; it was the reason she'd changed early and come out to listen.

"Of course you can write, silly." Madeline looked amused, as usual. "And I'll write back. We won't lose touch, I promise. And if you come back to Ashdown later, and I'm living close enough, I'll come to *your* graduation." Madeline was the only person to whom Eliza had mentioned this possibility. She didn't want Helen and Carrie to count on it.

> Those returning
> Those returning
> Make more faithful than before

Eliza sang in the middle of the long hot ceremony. The rain had held off, and the lush June foliage glittered in the dazzling light. Eliza squinted and Miss Tavistock, all dressed up in a flowered hat and a new suit, turned into a pink blur on the platform. The headmistress stood and gave a short address in memory of Miss Peck.

"My aunt's death is the end of a chapter. I have faith that all of the principles she stood for will be carried on by future Ashdown students. But the world is changing, and the school will have to meet the challenge of those changes."

"The end of a chapter," Eliza repeated to herself. Nothing would ever be the same.

She turned around and glimpsed Helen, half-dozing in the sun. It was the end of a chapter for the two of them as well. The strands of their fragile web of friendship seemed sturdy enough now, but they could break without constant replenishing. Eliza knew she would have to be the one to work at it.

Now the graduates were going up one at a time to get their certificates. Miss Tavistock looked proud of them. Eliza couldn't see her face, but the pink figure sat regally as she watched.

There was one more hymn, then three hundred and sixty voices chorused a loud "Amen." Eliza wiped her face. The sun was making her eyes water.

Other books by Kit Pearson

The Sky Is Falling

Winner of the Canadian Library Association Book of the Year Award for Children, the Mr. Christie's Award, and the Geoffrey Bilson Award for Historical Fiction for Young People.

It is the summer of 1940, and all of England fears an invasion by Hitler's army. Their parents decide to send Norah, ten, and Gavin, five, to safety. Norah, who thinks it's cowardly to go, hates the idea, but Gavin doesn't seem to mind.

In Toronto, they are taken into the luxurious house of the rich Ogilvie family. Gavin is thrilled, but Norah is miserable: Gavin doesn't seem to need her, the children at her new school tease her, and the news from England gets worse all the time.

But as Christmas approaches and Norah begins to make friends, she discovers a surprising responsibility that helps her accept her new country.

Looking at the Moon

Norah, an English "war guest" living with the wealthy Ogilvie family in Toronto, can hardly wait for August. She'll spend it at the Ogilvies' lavish cottage in Muskoka—a whole month of freedom, swimming, adventures with her "cousins"...

But this isn't an ordinary summer. It's 1943, and the war is still going on. Sometimes, Norah can't even remember what her parents look like —she hasn't seen them in three years. And she has turned thirteen, which means life seems to be getting more complicated.

Then a distant Ogilvie cousin, Andrew, arrives. He is nineteen, handsome, intelligent, and Norah thinks she may be falling in love for the first time. But Andrew has his own problems: he doesn't want to fight in the war, and yet he knows it's what his family and friends expect of him.

What the two of them learn from each other makes for a gentle, moving story, the second book in a trilogy that began with the award-winning *The Sky Is Falling*.

The Lights Go On Again

Winner of the National Chapter of Canada IODE Violet Downey Book Award

For five years Gavin and his sister Norah have lived in Canada as "war guests." But now, as 1945 approaches, the war is finally ending, and Gavin and Norah will soon be going back to England.

Norah, who's fifteen, is eager to see her parents again, but ten-year-old Gavin barely remembers them. He doesn't want to leave his Canadian family, his two best friends and his dog.

Then something happens that forces Gavin to make the most difficult decision of his life.

The Lights Go On Again is the last book in the acclaimed series that began with *The Sky Is Falling* and *Looking at the Moon*.

A Handful of Time

When Patricia's mother sends her to spend
the summer at her cousins' cottage out
west, Patricia doesn't want to go. She
doesn't know her cousins at all, and she's
never been good at camping or canoeing,
let alone making new friends.

When she arrives at the cottage, her worst
fears come true: Kelly, the girl she must share
a room with, teases her; Aunt Ginnie and Uncle
Doug feel sorry for her. She doesn't fit in.

Then Patricia discovers an old watch hidden
under a floorboard. When she winds it, she
finds herself taken back in time to the summer
when her own mother was twelve. As Patricia,
who's also twelve, travels back and forth
between past and present, she begins to
unlock the mystery of the old watch—and
of her troubled family.

Jenifer, Jamie, Emily,
Sydney, Monic,